Imperfections

Lori Bell

Copyright © 2015 by Lori Bell

Cover photograph by Lori Bell
Photographed on the cover, Michell Stockmann and her daughters, Kinsey and Kylie.

http://singleparents.about.com/od/legalissues/a/termination_parental_rights.htm
http://info.legalzoom.com/reverse-sole-custody-order-missouri-24250.html
http://www.lockwoodglen.com/our-homes?gclid=CLi9poXW7sUCFdcZgQod9nkAyQ
http://en.wikipedia.org/wiki/Gynecologic_hemorrhage#Definition
http://work.chron.com/job-description-secretary-construction-company-16483.
htmlhttp://oade.nd.edu/educate-yourself-alcohol/caution-alcohol-and-other-drugs-do-not-mix/ http://www.healthboards.com/boards/lung-respiratory-disorders-copd/395535-cardio-pulmonary-malfunction.html#ixzz3e7BnVcRW
http://www.projectknow.com/research/mixing-alcohol-and-sedatives/
http://www.drugfree.org/drug-guide/prescription-sedatives-tranquilizers/
https://en.wikipedia.org/wiki/Barbiturate_overdose
http://www.franklin-gov.com/government/parks/facilities-and-parks/park-locations-maps/park-locations/aspen-grove-park
https://books.google.com/books?id=plEsBQAAQBAJ&pg=PA941&lpg=PA941&dq=%E2%80%A2+Intravenous+administration+of+saline,+naloxone,+thiamine,+and/or+glucose.&source=bl&ots=38Q7_NKawc&sig=5HABo9Nyq1sxXu8W0QoZ5ShOpPU&hl=en&sa=X&ei=JtONVaK_MojjoATkqakQ&ved=0CDoQ6AEwBA#v=onepage&q=%E2%80%A2%20Intravenous%20administration%20of%20saline%2C%20naloxone%2C%20thiamine%2C%20and%2For%20glucose.&f=false http://californiafamilylawanddivorce.com/2012/05/18/do-california-courts-favor-mothers-in-child-custody-cases/

Printed by CreateSpace

ISBN 978-1515084396

DEDICATION

To my editing staff: Jen Flanagan, Erin Wagoner, and Kelly Ross. The three of you give me the confidence combined with constructive criticism to make this work seamlessly! I adore each of you for your individuality, your intellect, your talents, and your friendship. Thank you from the very bottom of my heart!

Chapter 1

She blew out the candles on the cake. There were not seventy-five individually lit candle wicks, only a number seven with a five beside it, both on top of the homemade chocolate cake, centered in the middle of the kitchen table.

It was hard to believe. Seventy-five. Where had the years gone? To the people, her family, gathered around the table now, she was mom, she was grandma. She was getting old. But, not to her. Not to Angie Roberts. She still felt much younger, although she had lived and experienced quite enough in her seventy-five years. More than most do in one lifetime.

As she looked around the table, Angie saw her children, in-laws, grandchildren, and one great grandbaby. They weren't a perfect family, dysfunctional was more like it, but they were hers. And she loved them. Each and every one of them.

When she was twenty-six years old, Angie gave birth to twin girls, Sadie and Sher. Her pregnancy was unplanned. She was only dating Dane Woods, the pharmaceutical rep she had met while working as an administrative assistant at a psychiatry office in St. Louis. She had never pondered settling down, getting married, and least of all, starting a family.

As if one baby weren't enough to tie her down and completely change her life, Angie had two. Dane was entirely more accepting of the shock. It was a life change, yes, but a blessing too, he had told Angie. She didn't see it that way, and it took her a very long time to realize her daughters were gifts.

Angie's twenty-five-year-old granddaughter, Jade stood behind her chair and wrapped her arms around her. She kissed her softly on the cheek and spoke aloud for everyone in the room to hear. "Happy Birthday, Gram. Love you to the moon and back." Angie smiled and tightly hugged her granddaughter's arms which were still folded across her chest. "Thank you, Jadey. Love you more." And she did. Angie loved all of her children and grandchildren alike, but she especially adored Jade.

Jade was Sher's daughter. Angie's fraternal twins, Sadie and Sher, were like night and day, oil and water. Complete opposites. Sadie was kind, compassionate and selfless. She had two teenage sons who were exactly like her. Sher was often bitter, self-centered most of the time, and she had one daughter, Jade who was exactly like her grandmother. Angie and Jade were two of a kind, fifty years apart in age but their souls were one in the same.

2

The cake was eaten as Angie picked up the rectangular glass pan from the center of the table and carried it over to the counter top near the sink. She had a window above the sink which she caught herself intently looking out of for a moment. She watched Jade sitting alone, outside on the wooden bench swing near the detached garage with yellow siding to match the house. Her granddaughter had that same look in her eyes which Angie remembered seeing in the mirror when she was her age. She was broken inside.

Angie watched Jade's husband, Rhett Connors walk over to her and then he stood near the swing. He was holding their six-month-old baby girl, Aspen. He was always the one to hold her, take care of her, and love her. Jade remained detached, and Angie's eyes welled up with tears as she watched them from the window.

It was like yesterday in her own mind. She and Dane Woods were married by a Justice of the Peace at City Hall in O'Fallon, Illinois. It wasn't romantic and hardly memorable as Angie stood in front of a man who loved her with all he had. She was seven months pregnant, wearing what felt like a white tent dress, and trying to get into the moment of pledging her love and her life to a man whom she was not entirely sure she would have wanted to call her husband if she had not been about to have his babies. She didn't have to marry him, she knew that, but she did anyway.

And that's when she began to feel broken inside. It was supposed to be *her* life. *She* had plans to study psychiatry. That was her passion. Not her husband, and not even her twin baby girls.

Angie never embraced her babies with the intent of bonding with them and loving them with her entire being as most mothers do. She never kissed them with feeling while inhaling their sweet baby scent. She never held their little hands with the intention of seizing that moment by recognizing how fast time goes by, how those little fingers and toes are not small for very long. She just went through the motions for an entire year, and on the eve of their first birthday, Angie packed one suitcase full of clothes and a few other things, and she left her family. Her husband begged her not to abandon their baby girls. He told her if it was him she could not live with, he would divorce her, they could co-parent, but *please do not leave your babies.*

Dane stood in the doorway of the nursery and watched his wife positioned in between the two cribs, angled on the white shag carpet in the middle of the room. Only a nightlight plugged into a wall socket dimly lit up the room. She took a deep breath as she could feel her heart pounding inside of her chest. She whispered, "be good for your daddy," and she turned and walked away. She didn't feel the emotions right then and there that she should have felt walking away from her own flesh and blood, and not knowing if she would ever see them again. Dane, however, felt all of it for her, for himself, and especially for their daughters. He had the pangs of panic and a rush of tears flooded his eyes and his face. She walked by him, and stopped. He was a good man. He was an amazing father to their babies. He would be okay. She trusted that, and moreover she trusted him with the lives of her babies. They were his babies now. "You've got this, Dane." It was cold, it was heartless, but Angie never felt more certain about anything. Leaving was the right thing to do. For herself. She needed to save herself, and she believed abandoning her family was the only way to do it.

And now, a half of a century later, she was witnessing the same pain, the same torment, plaguing her granddaughter. It was true, those sayings that go around. *It runs in the family. The apple doesn't fall far from the tree. It must be in her genes.* Jade

4

Connors was her grandmother, all over again. She was five-foot-five with long, golden blonde hair and a curvy size six figure. She was wild, spontaneous, and forthright. And so easy to love. Rhett Connors, also twenty-five years old, walked into a bar on State Street in the City of O'Fallon and took one look at the blonde beauty serving drinks and flashing more than a smile behind the bar. He fell harder for her than she did for him. And when she got pregnant, he wanted to marry her. She agreed, but not wholeheartedly.

Angie watched that young man holding his baby girl in his arms walk away from the swing in the backyard and toward his small charcoal gray pickup truck parked near the garage. He placed the baby in her car seat in the cramped backseat behind the driver's seat. After he buckled her up safely, he closed the door. Angie had the kitchen window cracked open now and she heard Rhett call out to his wife. "Jade…are you coming or not?" She never answered him. She just got up off of the swing and walked over to the pickup truck and got in on the passenger side. Her body language spoke volumes. Slumped shoulders. Head hanging low. She was miserable. She never buckled her seatbelt after she slammed the truck door shut and stared straight ahead. Watching her scared the life out of Angie. She would not be able to live with herself if she allowed her grand-daughter to make the same mistake as she had.

Angie closed the kitchen window and turned around with her lower back resting against the counter top in front of the sink. At seventy-five, Angie looked damn good. In the last fifty years she had aged, but she looked far from her age. She still wore her clothing fitted and she still made an effort to rejuvenate her body every day with some form of activity or exercise. She had gone up only two dress sizes over the years and she was proud of her physical appearance. You would not find her wearing old lady elastic pants or oversized flowered blouses. No. Angie donned jeans, t-shirts, lower cut blouses than most ladies her age would dare to wear, and when she dressed up, she wore skirts or dresses to the knee and a little above to show off her toned legs. Now, she stood in her kitchen, wearing a long-sleeved light blue denim button-down shirt rolled up to her elbows, with a pair of white capri jeans and yellow flip flops on her feet. Her nails on her toes and her fingers were painted cherry red. She wore makeup on her face, mascara on her eyelashes, and her once long, golden blonde hair was now cut two inches above her neckline and she frequented her hairstylist regularly to keep sporting white blonde hair. Her face was not spared from Father Time. She had laugh lines and crow's-feet and even a few deeper wrinkles, but every face told a story and if every feature could speak there would be tales of pain, loneliness, sorrow and regret. But, to Angie's credit, she had always embraced the trying times as well as the good. Throughout it all, she persevered. In her lifetime, she had also felt happiness, accomplished, cared for, needed, and loved. It had just taken too many years for her to reach the point where she loved herself, and accepted imperfection.

Chapter 2

It was dark outside as Angie was driving down State Street in O'Fallon. Just as she had expected, she saw Jade's pickup truck parked under the street light at Shooters, a bar on the corner of State and Lincoln. She and Rhett only had one vehicle, because it was all they could afford. He worked at Spengler Plumbing during the day and she tended bar at night. With a baby at home, the bar was no place for Jade to be every night, Angie thought to herself, as she pulled into the parking lot behind the bar and found an open space to park her compact white Lincoln MKZ.

She was still wearing her yellow flip flops and white denim capris with the sleeves now rolled down on her blue denim shirt. As she pulled open the door to the bar, she flashed back to all the years of her life spent in places like this. It couldn't be any different for Jade to feel at home there, it was in her blood, Angie reflected, as she made eye contact with her granddaughter the moment she stepped foot onto that sticky bar room floor.

Jade, looking wide-eyed, walked swiftly around the bar and met her in the middle of the floor. "Gram, what you are doing here?" Jade was wearing tight dark-washed jeans and her cleavage was spilling out of a black tank top with Shooters spelled out on the front in neon green.

"You know I'm no stranger to bars, honey," Angie said winking at her granddaughter, who felt like she should be embarrassed but she wasn't. She adored her grandmother and she connected with her more than she ever had with anyone else.

"Can I get you a beer, Gram?"

"A longneck, please," Angie replied, tucking her arm into Jade's and the two of them walked up to the bar.

Jade waited on two more customers after she gave Angie a beer in a bottle. While Angie sat there, sipping her beer, she let her mind wander to when she was in her prime and spending so much of her time in the bars. She was very wild with the men and Angie smirked at those memories as Jade caught her expression.

"Strolling down memory lane?" Jade asked Angie. She could read her. They could read each other. Again, it was as if they shared the same soul. Jade admired her grandmother more than words could express. She knew her history, her struggles, her triumphs, and she trusted her above anyone else.

"I was *all that* back in my day, Jadey," Angie said, sighing and wanting to curse how fast the time had gone. Her body was aging, but her heart and her mind still felt so vibrant.

"I'm sure you were, Gram. You're still hot," Jade said, resting her elbows on the bar top in front of Angie, allowing only inches between their faces.

"Damn right I am," Angie agreed, letting out a hoarse laugh as she finished the last swallow of beer left in the bottle, and added, "Do you have time to talk? You know we need to." Jade walked around from behind the bar and sat down on a stool right next to Angie.

"You always could read me, Gram," Jade began, with tears welling up in her eyes. "I'm not happy. I am trying, really trying, to be a good mother and a good wife. I want to love Aspen, I do. I want to be like all of those other mothers who don't care how their life is no longer their own. I want to get drunk on her love, her scent, her smile... but I can't. I just can't."

"I understand, Jadey. You know I do." Angie reached out for her granddaughter and Jade fell into her arms.

***

Angie spent four years away from her family. She left when her twin girls were babies, only one-year-old, and she had not seen them again until they were five. She ran away from her responsibilities as a mother and her commitment to her husband. She didn't go far, only twenty-five miles west to St. Louis. She grew up there and she had spent most of her young adulthood living in a studio apparent in the heart of the city. She returned to that life, the life where she had felt she was the most happy and free. She wanted to enroll at St. Louis University again. It was the college she attended for only one semester before she became pregnant. She wanted to delve back into the way her life was before she was pregnant and rushed to get married. And so she did.

Angie had kept the severance pay from her bosses at the psychiatry office. She had it in a bank in St. Louis and never shared it with Dane. His salary as a pharmaceutical rep had allowed them to move into a previously owned home in the Fairwood Hills subdivision in O'Fallon. It was a comfortable life. They had the means to get the nursery ready for twins, buying double of everything. Angie should have been happy and excited to begin a new life, but she wasn't. She wanted no part of being a wife and a mother to two babies. And that is why, after one year, she left.

Angie could still remember what it felt like when she got into her car, packed with only one suitcase and just a few other things she wanted to take with her, and drove onto Interstate 64 and never looked back.

She ignored the calls from Dane, her mother, his mother. She just wanted to be left alone to make an effort to move forward with her life, without feeling the pull to come back. She felt the guilt and she did miss her babies, at first. But, as time went by, Angie made a life for herself as a college student by day and a bartender at night.

She attended St. Louis University where she studied to become a psychiatrist. The classes reeled her in, and she knew that field was her calling. Eventually, Angie allowed minimal contact with her mother. She told her she was living in St. Louis again and working toward earning a psychiatry degree. And Angie would never forget her mother's response. *Leave it to the sick in the head to feel called to help the other mental cases out there.* Angie's mother accused her of failing as a wife and mother the day she abandoned her family. Angie listened, but she never responded on the opposite end of the phone.

As if that phone call was not bad enough to replay in her mind, Angie also received a call from Dane the same day. Obviously her mother had notified him about Angie's whereabouts.

"I'm surprised you answered this time," was the first thing Dane spoke to her.

"Hello, Dane," Angie replied into the opposite end of the phone.

"It's been seven months since you left, how much longer are you going to go on like this?" Dane would have waited for his wife forever. He worshipped her. Despite the fact that she broke his heart and abandoned their babies, Dane Woods would have taken her back. He loved her that much, and he wanted more than anything to give his babies their mother back.

"I have a new life now," Angie tried to explain. "It's good. It's all good. I hope you can say the same," Angie momentarily held her breath as she awaited his answer. She could only imagine the stress he was under being a single father to two babies as he worked full-time.

"Good isn't the word I would use to describe my life," he replied. "It's been hell juggling it all, but what other choice did I have? You left. I have a full-time nanny for the girls and our moms help out a lot. I want you back, Ang!" Just like that, he exclaimed exactly how he felt. "I'm mad as hell at you for what you did, but I love you and I need you and any anger or bitterness that I've carried suddenly diminished when I heard your voice again on this phone."

"I can't, Dane. I want a divorce. We both have a right to move on with our lives." She felt pained knowing she was hurting him all over again, seven months after she left him, but she needed her freedom and in time he would understand how he did as well.

Dane never agreed to divorce her, so Angie never pressed the issue. She just continued to live her life separate from her husband and their babies. Four years went by. Angie had earned a Bachelor of Science degree and she attended her graduation ceremony alone. She watched the people who surrounded her that day. She saw the other graduates celebrating with their families. Parents were proud, and taking pictures. Spouses were hugging and kissing, and some children were in the mix as well. That was when it hit Angie. She had those people in her life. She could have attained her goals with them all still intact. It had never occurred to her to alter her expectations a bit. Maybe attend school at night when Dane was able to watch the babies. For someone who was studying mental health and planned to continue on to earn her medical degree and eventually work in residency, Angie suddenly felt foolish, and regret finally began to set in.

But, instead of running back to a man who wanted to resume a life with her and to her babies who were still young enough to forgive and forget, Angie did what she knew best. She walked into the bar on the Central West End in St. Louis and she ordered a drink. It was the very same bar where she worked for the past four years. There were familiar faces and there were some strangers too. That night, Angie took another stranger back to her studio apartment. She didn't feel worthy of her family anymore. Too much time had passed.

Her cap and gown were still hanging on the back of the bathroom door. It had only been two days since Angie received her diploma, a degree which she was incredibly proud to have earned. A knock on her apartment door left Angie dumfounded when she opened it to find her mother standing on the other side. It had been four years since she had seen her, as well.

And that's when her mother told her it was time to come home. She had no choice this time. She was beside herself because Dane was in a car accident and it was not likely that he would live. Angie was crushed. She was not going to be forced to take a different path in her life just because of the unfairness of this turn of events. No. She could not possibly be a mother to two five-year-old little girls now. Her girls. But, would they even remember her?

She never had the chance to tell her mother *no, absolutely not*, because the next thing she witnessed nearly brought her to her knees. She had never invited her mother inside of her studio apartment. She stood inside, holding the door open for her mother outside. She saw the back door of her mother's car fling open and two little girls got out. One of the two was more eager to run, while the other trailed behind.

The little girl who took the lead, passed up her grandmother and immediately made her way to Angie. She never hesitated to wrap her arms around Angie's waist and upper legs.

Angie was uncertain if she was Sadie or Sher, the names she had given her twin daughters at birth. Both of them had long hair with natural curls, one was blonde and the other brunette, with round faces with big brown eyes. Time had passed quickly. They had gone from babies to five-year-old little girls and Angie, their own mother, did not know them at all.

She wrapped her arms around the child and then froze. This was it. This was what she had begged for four years ago. To feel the love. To feel the connection. To not be able to breathe because she loved her children that much. That feeling was there, evident and strong. And then she heard the child, her child, speak. "Gramma says you're coming home with us."

Angie glared at her mother first and then eased her expression as she looked down at the little girl still standing so close to her and then at the other one who chose to stay near her grandmother.

"She does not want us," the little girl, with dark hair, standing farthest from her spoke. "Face it, Sadie. She abandoned us." It was like a knife piercing through her heart.

14

That was Angie's first experience dealing with Sher, the daughter who would be bitter and unforgiving for a very long time. Sadie, however, defended her mother.

"Gramma said what's done is done and to get over it!" Angie found herself smiling at Sadie's reply to her sister. My goodness, she had missed out on so much. And she could feel the pull, back to them, as she stood there. It was intense, unbelievably powerful. She wanted to know them. She realized she had loved them, just not enough to want to stay. And that decision had finally began to chip away at her heart.

The twins lost their father the same day they reunited with their mother. Dane Woods succumbed to injuries from a car accident at the age of thirty. The investigation was inconclusive, but the autopsy did confirm head and neck injuries as the cause of death. Although it could not be determined, it was assumed he had fallen asleep at the wheel when he crossed the center line and tragically collided with an oncoming car.

Dane's death was a prime example of how only the good die young. The loss of his life would have a rippling effect on all of their lives for many years to come.

***

Jade pulled out of her grandmother's embrace. Her face was wet with tears and her eyes illustrated a pain Angie had seen in the mirror five decades ago. "You listen to me, Jadey, and you listen damn good. This will pass. You have to hang in there. Do not make the same ludicrous mistake as I did."

"I know the story, Gram, but I need for you to talk to me, really talk to me, about it now. Throughout my entire childhood, my mom harped about you leaving and there were times I know she hated you for it." Jade was desperate to reach out to Angie for guidance. She was the only one who truly understood what was going through her body, mind, and soul right now.

Angie sighed before speaking. She wished she had more beer in the bottle sitting on the bar in front of her right now. This was not going to be easy. "As much as your mother got over it, she didn't really get over it. My leaving scarred her as deeply as her father's death. Life shit on my girls from the very start and it's a wonder they turned out as well as they did."

"You gave them a good life when you came back, Gram," Jade defended her.

"I did, and I certainly strived to make up for the pain and loneliness I caused and for all of the time I missed," Angie explained. "But, the damage was always there. It was thrown back in my face many times as I raised my girls. And, now, watching you as a young mother, I'm scared, Jadey. I see so much of myself in you and I swear to you, I will not stop, I will take my last breath trying to pull you out of this quicksand."

Tears were spilling from Jade's eyes again. "Just hold me, Gram. Hold me until this feeling goes away."

Another half an hour had passed and it was near closing time. Only two men were left sitting on the opposite end of the bar from Angie and Jade. When Jade offered to walk her grandmother out to her car in the dark parking lot, Angie agreed after she made her promise to go home soon to her family.

When Jade stepped back inside of the bar, she noticed a man had come in while she was outside. She saw him from behind before she walked around the bar to tell him it was almost closing time. He was wearing tight faded denim, brown worn cowboy boots, a pressed olive green oxford shirt, and a brown cowboy hat which was sun bleached and tattered around the edging. When she made her way behind the bar, he took off his cowboy hat and she saw more of his face and his eyes bore into hers. "Hello darlin', is it too late to grab a beer?" His voice was masculine but gentle with an evident southern accent. His dark hair, a little matted from his hat, was growing out a bit on the sides and bangs and it looked damp from a shower or product.

"We are about to close," Jade answered, finding herself immediately wishing she had not said that.

"I happen to drink fast, so could I just get one?" The man straddled a stool directly in front of where Jade was standing. Only the bar separated the two of them and Jade had this feeling she couldn't describe. She smiled and filled up a tall, thick-rimmed glass with beer and set it down on the bar top in front of him. He reached for the glass just as she was pulling her hand away and his fingers lightly brushed hers.

"I'm Brock," he said. "I'm Jade," she said in response.

"Nice to meet you, Jade. I appreciate the beer." He tipped back the glass and downed half of it before speaking again. "So what's your story? Are you attached?" Brock was being forthright and Jade looked down at her left hand, the hand on which she should have been wearing her wedding band, but she never wore it when she worked.

"No," she answered abruptly, "I'm not." She now had taken a dangerous step in defiance of what her grandmother had just warned her against.

Chapter 3

Angie dreamt about Dane that night after she left Jade at the bar. She tossed and turned all throughout her sleep as she saw his face and relived beginning again with her twins following their father's tragic death.

She moved back into their ranch-style camel brown brick home in the Fairwood Hills subdivision. It was strange being in Dane's bedroom, knowing he had lived there, slept there, most likely alone for the past four years. She wondered if he had been faithful, he didn't have to be. She certainly had not been. In her mind, they were divorced. She knew Dane well, he was an incredibly loyal man, and she believed he was holding out hope for her to return one day.

Her return was forced, but it felt right. It finally had felt true and real to Angie to be a mother to her children. She pushed aside her dream to become a psychiatrist, and she used her bachelor's degree to find a good job. She fell into a real estate career and actually enjoyed it while she made a decent living for herself and her girls. A roof over their heads, finances under control, and togetherness fell into place. Adjustment, getting to know each other, and learning to love were, however, incredibly challenging. Sometimes Angie thought she would never get there with Sher. Sadie was the daughter who took after her father. She was kind-hearted and forgiving just like Dane. Sher was the stubborn, bitter, self-centered one, similar to her mother.

Angie was gentle when she needed to be and stern when she had to be with both of her girls. She found herself pushing too hard concerning Sher. Sher was an unhappy child and continued to be until she was a teenager. Then, she became rebellious and damn near out of control. And Angie lost control with her the night of the twins' sixteenth birthday. That was the night Sher stayed out hours past her curfew and Angie discovered she lost her virginity to a boy she hardly knew.

After Angie screamed at her until her voice was nearly lost and her throat ached, she sat down beside her wide-eyed daughter on their living room couch and fought back the tears as she told Sher something she had never before told anyone. Something she had never realized herself until she had to raise her daughters and witness their pain and anguish, especially Sher's. Losing their father, their only parent, at such a young age had affected Sher the very same way losing her own father at the age of nine had scarred Angie.

"I lost my daddy, too," Angie began, and Sher listened raptly. "I was nine. He was my whole world. You know that saying, *she thought he hung the moon*, well my God I believed that man did."

Sher knew her grandfather died at a very young age from a heart attack, but she never knew the repercussions his death had on her mother. And Angie held nothing back this time when she told her how her life spiraled out of control for many years and carried into her adulthood.

Angie admitted how she craved attention from men. She confessed to living in bars and picking up strangers and taking them home. Sex was her escape and she begged her daughter not to follow that same destructive path. Angie painted an unflattering picture of herself for her daughter, but she did it purposely to instill fear in her and forewarn her how it could happen to her, too. She told her how when she finally found a man who adored her, loved her unconditionally, she couldn't love him in return because she never felt deserving of him. She had not loved and respected herself first. Angie did not make excuses for her past behavior, but she turned her heart inside out that night when she spoke to her daughter. They came to a new understanding then. Sher began to open up to the idea of accepting and respecting her mother. Loving her came many years later. And then hating her inevitably found its way back in the last decade, as Sher recognized how her own daughter was becoming just like her grandmother. Genes had paved the way for destruction and Sher felt as if there was absolutely nothing at all she could do to stop it.

After restless sleep and awaking worry-filled for Jade, Angie made her way out to the wooden bench swing in her backyard with a cup of coffee in hand. She was already dressed in a pair of khaki Bermuda shorts and a pale yellow v-neck cotton shirt and her hair was done as well as her makeup applied. Her feet were bare as she padded through the grass and sat down on the swing. She had only taken a couple of sips of her coffee before she noticed a car pulling into her driveway. Her daughter, Sher was paying her an early morning visit before she went to work. Sher Woll was the principal of a grade school in O'Fallon District 90. She took her job seriously and at fifty years old she dreaded the day she would have to retire. Those children, their education, and their success meant the world to her. Sher, in a cream-colored cropped pantsuit with heels to match, made her way over to the swing to her mother.

"Good morning," Angie said first.

"Aren't you going to ask what brings me here so early?" Sher seemed miffed as she remained standing in the grass near the swing.

"No, because I know you will skip the *how are you doing this morning, mother* chatter and tell me," Angie smirked behind her mug and she carefully sipped the hot coffee.

Sher folded her long arms across her chest and pointed one of her heels out in front of her in the grass. She was built long and lean, like her father. She even had his dark hair. Her natural color at age fifty was flaked with an abundance of gray, so she regularly had it colored more auburn than her dark, natural color. In a way, Sher now reminded Angie of her old friend, MJ Payne. MJ was her boss once upon a time when Angie worked as an administrative assistant for a psychiatry firm in St. Louis. MJ was her best friend for a few years and then they lost touch. Last Angie had heard, probably forty-something years ago, MJ had married her business partner, Sam Brewster and the two of them ended up having four children.

"I went for a walk late last night, downtown, and I passed Shooters just in time to see my daughter leaning up against her pickup truck, talking to a cowboy, hat and all. She didn't see me, and it's no wonder because even with only the street lights shining, I could see she was taken by him."

Angie knew there had not been a cowboy present in the bar when she was there, late. She had hoped Jade made her way home to her family after closing time. "I'm sure it was harmless," Angie said in her granddaughter's defense, as she concealed her worry.

"Stop, mom. Stop taking Jade's side. You know she's in trouble! I can't seem to reach her, no matter what I say or do, but what else is new?" Sher uncrossed her arms and stood straighter with her heels together. "But, you can."

"I'm trying," Angie admitted, sincerely.

"And do you feel like she's responding to you at all?"

"I went to the bar last night, to Shooters," Angie clarified, "to see Jadey." Sher stopped herself from rolling her eyes. She hated how her mother meshed well in a bar, any bar. She still resented that about her because she knew her mother's past. "We had a heart-to-heart. She and I, we connect, we get each other," Angie said to her daughter.

"Exactly, mom, so fucking save her from this downward spiral!" Sher was angry and adamant and more than a little bit desperate.

"I will do whatever it takes. I promise you, I will." And that was all Angie said before Sher walked away. She muttered *thank you* under her breath before she turned on her heels and left.

***

It took three knocks, one a little bit louder than the other, before Jade answered the door of her small home with powder blue siding on the north side of O'Fallon. It was an established area of a growing city, in which thirty thousand residents lived.

"Gram, hi, come in. Sorry, I was changing the baby's diaper." Jade looked disheveled in her cut-off, overly frayed white jean shorts and revealing solid gray, ribbed tank top. Her hair was in a knot on top of her head and she wasn't wearing any makeup.

Angie stepped into her house and noticed the disarray immediately. Laundry was piled up on the sofa in the living room, plates of half-eaten food were on the coffee table, the TV was blaring, and the floor looked like it needed to be vacuumed. But, with a baby, sometimes things did not get cleaned up or put away. Angie understood that, and then she asked where the baby was.

"In her crib," Jade replied. "It's good for her to have some alone time, and cry it out if it comes to that." Angie disagreed. This was a time when Jade should have wanted to be with her baby and she should have been spoiling her by now, picking her up after every whimper. This scared Angie, because she remembered a time when she acted the same way throughout the first year of her babies' lives. That memory sickened her now.

"Go get her. I want to hold her," Angie told Jade and she obliged. She returned a few minutes later with the baby in her arms. Aspen's back, neck, and head were strong as she held herself upright while Jade carried her into the living room. And, as soon as Angie took the baby from her, she smelled urine and felt the soaked the diaper through her sleeper. "I thought you said you changed her," Angie spoke outright, knowing better, knowing this baby was not being well taken care of by her mother.

"I guess she peed again. Damn, what a waste of diapers. Those things are expensive, too." Jade complained and made no effort to change the baby, so Angie walked out of the room and to the nursery. Someone had to tend to the baby's needs.

When she returned to the living room, Jade was texting on her cell phone. "Are you talking to that cowboy who waltzed in Shooters last night after I left?" Angie was always direct, and made no apologies for it.

"What?" Jade played dumb.

"Someone I know was walking by last night and saw you engrossed in conversation outside in the parking lot," Angie explained.

"My mother," Jade sighed. "She's the only one who walks the streets that late at night. I know she purposely takes the downtown route to check up on me."

"She should," Angie defended her daughter, "because you keep giving her reasons to worry." The baby was chewing on a soft rattle Angie had given her from her crib, and Angie sat down with her on the laundry-free end of the sofa. Jade was sitting in the recliner chair, adjacent to her.

"She's just mad at me again because I've disappointed her," Jade rolled her eyes, pretending it didn't hurt to not be close to her mother.

"You have not disappointed anyone," Angie tried to reassure her granddaughter. "This is a rough patch and you will make it through. You have no other choice. This baby needs you, and your husband, too. He adores you."

"Were you ever in love, Gram? I mean, really in love with chemistry, passion, and all that undeniable shit you only read about in books or see in the movies?"

Angie momentarily allowed herself to be distracted by Aspen in her arms. And then she replied, "I was once. It was instantaneous and passionate from the beginning. All he had to do was look at me, and I was done in. But, honey, that kind of feeling, call it love, call it infatuation, does not last."

"Tell me who he was," Jade asked her.

"He was a man with an ulterior motive. He wanted to get close to me in order to hurt my best friend at the time. I ran my mouth too much, drinking and flirting, and I got myself and my best friend into some trouble. That man ended up kidnapping his biological son and framing my best friend." Jade looked puzzled as she was trying to comprehend the complex story. "It all turned out alright for the child, but what I'm getting at here is no matter how he made me feel or how in love I was with him, it wasn't real. What's real is the way your husband looks at you and this baby the two of you have created. Family is everything. Don't be young and stupid like I was."

"Gram, I know, okay?" Jade said those words but Angie didn't believe her.

***

Later, when Angie was alone again, she found herself going there in her mind. To the past. To the years she spent alone, without a man. Angie was a strong woman, she never needed a life partner. And she never had one. Dane was the only man she married, but she didn't love him. Mark Wise was the only man she truly loved. And he was the man who deceived her, as she had told Jade. The more Angie thought about love and being in love and getting swept up in all of it, she began to wonder if she had given Jade the wrong advice. Should she really stay with a man she does not love? Angie was seventy-five years old and alone. Time had flown by and she spent those years raising her daughters and finally meeting their needs. Year after year, Angie put herself on the back-burner. She never took the time to date or allow herself to meet anyone and fall in love. The inner psychiatrist in her knew she had punished herself through the years. She had gone from selfish to selfless, but she brought being selfless to an extreme level. She deserved to be loved and happy, too. She just never chased that dream. And, now, she wondered if she was doing the right thing with Jade.

Angie wouldn't allow herself another similar thought. Just because she had, time and again, perceived herself as a lonely old fool, she was not going to stand by and watch Jade make a mistake she would regret for the rest of her life. And then she retracted her thought about being a lonely *old* fool. Seventy-five was not old and she refused to let a thought such as that sink into her mind. Angie Roberts had a lot of living left to do.

Chapter 4

Shooters was bustling and Jade was in the zone. Serving the customers. Keeping her mind on anything but the draining, depressive day she had at home, alone with her baby girl. She was disgusted with herself for feeling that way, every day, and working at the popular bar downtown O'Fallon each night was her escape. She felt at home there. She didn't feel judged or ridiculed.

The hours behind the bar flew by as they did every night, and just before closing time he walked in again. The bar room was only about half full and Jade spotted him as soon as he came in the door. He was a man with that kind of presence. He held the scene. Captivated the room. Again, he looked like a cowboy. Tight jeans. Worn boots. That tattered hat pulled just low enough above his eyes. He was wearing a white, starched shirt tonight as he strolled toward the bar and directly up to Jade.

"You own this place or just run it like you do?" He smiled as he spoke to her and she returned one to him. Jade was wearing a short, black skirt with a full ruffled-hem and she too was wearing a white, button down shirt. Her sleeves were rolled up and the buttons on the chest were open dangerously low. She was wearing black wedges tonight which heightened her five-foot frame closer to Brock at five-foot-nine.

"If I owned it, I'd have my feet up in the corner with a drink in my hand," Jade responded, wishing for a moment like that later tonight. More often than not, she had a drink or two, alone, after hours in the bar. It was better than going home. The longer she stayed at work, the better her chances were to find Rhett asleep when she came home. She no longer wanted to hear him complain about their lack of family time when he was in a bad mood. Nor did she want to respond to his advances when he was in a good mood. It wasn't the life she envisioned for herself. She wasn't at all happy.

"Have a beer with me," Brock suggested as he straddled the bar stool on the end, a little further away from the crowd and Jade instantly felt like the two of them were the only ones in the room. He had that affect on her, already.

"Stick around for closing time," she replied as she slowly slid his glass of beer toward him and he reached for it and flashed a smile at her.

Thirty-five minutes later the bar was empty, the open sign in the window was unlit, and Jade walked over to the door to lock it. When she turned around, she saw Brock from across the room, now standing behind the bar. He was getting her a beer, on tap. "Sit down, put your feet up and have that beer with me."

Jade found a table against a far wall. She sat down, carefully in her short ruffled skirt and crossed her toned, shapely legs. Brock walked to her table, placed two beers down on it, and pulled one of the chairs closer to hers. They both took a few sips before either one of them spoke.

"So what brings you back here?" Jade asked him, not really knowing him as they had not shared much personal information the first night they met.

"I like this place, and its company," Brock smiled.

"Oh, I didn't see you socializing with its company, cowboy," Jade teased and she got a laugh out of him.

"It only takes one person to bring me back somewhere," he said, sincerely.

"Where are you from, Brock Cowboy?" Jade asked him, feeling like she wanted to know more. His last name, included.

"Franklin, Tennessee, very close to Nashville," he replied. "And, my name is Brock Green." He then told Jade how he was a construction worker, out of Tennessee and he and his crew were working in O'Fallon at a site on Scott Air Force Base. Their project was planned for six months, and he was staying in a hotel just off of Interstate 64.

"So you're here, away from home, for the next six months?" Jade asked him, wondering if that was a good thing. She shouldn't be getting to know another man. She knew better, but she didn't care. And that frightened her, a little, but intrigued her more.

"At least," he answered.

It was two in the morning and many beers later before Jade said she really needed to get home. She didn't say that her husband's alarm sounds at four-fifteen for his work day. In fact, she didn't offer much at all about herself and her life throughout their endless conversation tonight. Brock mostly told her more about himself and the two of them just talked about life. It had been a very long time since Jade truly embraced conversation with someone other than her grandmother. Angie had a way of reaching Jade, really getting her to think and feel, and Brock Green had now done the same.

Brock helped Jade clean up the bar and he waited for her to turn off the lights and retrieve her handbag and keys from the backroom. She locked the door from the outside and then he walked her around the building to the parking lot. She saw his big, silver diesel truck parked next to her old, small, charcoal gray pickup which she shared with her husband. "And there sits my tiny truck next to your enormous, own-the-road one."

He smiled at her in the dark, again with only the street light shining, and then she spoke. "Thank you for your company tonight, Brock Green. It was nice. Come back again, if you want. God knows I'll be here."

"The pleasure was all mine, Jade," he said, realizing he still didn't know her last name. She was very much a mystery to him and he looked forward to getting to know her better.

She smiled at him and opened the door to her pickup. He stepped a little closer to her and met her behind the open door. Again, in her wedges she noticed how she nearly met his height. He placed both of his hands on her hips and inched his body a little closer to hers. She felt something. A connection. A rush of adrenaline. Tingles from his touch. She had not felt that way in a very long time, if ever. She wasn't thinking as she met her lips with his and instantly got lost in the feel of being kissed with undeniable passion. Their lips were still wet from the beer, and she could taste the salt from the pretzels he had been eating on the table they sat at for hours. One kiss felt endless, and moments later they were both breathless.

"Good night, Jade," his voice was quiet and a little raspy.

"Yes it has been a good night," she replied, "and I wish it didn't have to end." She was treading dangerously with that comment and she knew it.

"Don't you worry, the night may be ending, but not us. We are just beginning." His words took her by surprise.

"What makes you so sure?" she asked, craving that reassurance. Nothing was for certain in her life anymore, at least nothing felt as if it was.

"I was certain, from the moment you told me your name." Jade was listening raptly. "Jade, by definition, is a green stone." He smiled at her as she watched her eyes widen under the dark sky.

"Good night, Mr. Green." she replied, feeling as if the stars in a very dark sky high above her were finally aligned.

***

Jade walked past the yellow garage and up to the swing in her grandmother's yard. She could always find her there when she needed her. Angie had been mowing her lawn and picking the weeds out of her flower garden before she sat down with a glass of sweet tea. She enjoyed her modest home and yard just off of Smiley Street, north of Estelle Kampmeyer Grade School, where her children attended many years ago. Being in real estate for thirty years was challenging and fulfilling for her, and she learned as the years progressed how it was okay to leave a house with memories behind. Once her children were grown, Angie moved out of the home she always considered to be Dane's. It was too far out of town and too spacious for just her living there, so she downsized.

She saw Jade walking up her driveway, no pickup truck and no baby. Angie watched her before she spoke. She seemed more put together than she had in awhile. She looked as if she put some effort into pressing her clothes and matching an outfit. She was wearing stone-washed chino shorts, with a very short hem, a peach cap-sleeved lycra shirt with a generous scoop neck, and brown boat shoes with zebra prints on the sides.

"Hi Gram, I thought I'd find you here," Jade said, as Angie noticed a light in her eyes.

"You can find me anywhere, anytime, you know that," Angie reassured her granddaughter. "Come sit, I can get you a sweet tea if you'd like?"

"No, I'm good. You're all the sweet I need, Gram." Angie put her arm around Jade and pulled her close.

"So, no truck, and more importantly, no baby?" Angie asked her.

"Rhett is working so he has the truck, and I hired our neighbor girl for a few hours. Aspen has really taken to her." Angie wished her own mother would take to her, but she knew all too well how feelings could not be forced. She tried to force herself, time and again, and then she just completely gave up and left. "I need to tell you something, Gram. I didn't get home until almost three in the morning last night, Rhett was furious because the baby wouldn't sleep and he had to get up and ready for work at four. I just told him I was at the bar alone again and had extra things to take care of after closing time." Jade was still

on a high from spending the wee hours of the morning with
Brock Green. She had not forgotten what he said to her either.
She knew it wasn't a pickup line, she had heard them all before.
This man was genuine and the feelings she had when she was
with him could not have felt anymore real. "That cowboy came
back. His name is Brock Green. We talked for hours. We have a
connection, already, Gram. I don't know how to explain it. I just
feel like I have a purpose when I'm with him."

"People are going to start talking, Jadey. You're in a
public place. This may be a growing city, but it has never lost its
small-town feel, and in small towns gossip thrives. Everyone
knows everyone else and their business. How are you going to
explain this to your husband?" Angie was worried, but she was
not going to be critical, because again she related all too well.

"Rhett has not felt like my husband in a very long time.
I'm not sure he ever has. I don't know the last time he's touched
me, or when I've wanted him to." Jade was looking down at her
feet as the swing they were sitting on remained stationary.

"Did you sleep with Brock Green?" Angie asked her
outright, believing she had last night.

"No, but he did kiss me," Jade replied, "and I can tell you
I've never been so swept away in my life. No passion has ever
seeped into my soul. Not for anything, and especially not for a
man. Not until Brock Green."

Angie just sat there for a moment. She made no attempt
to sip the sweet tea in the glass that was sweating in her hand
and resting on her lap, and she spoke no words yet. She would
not be judgmental. She would offer advice, if she could, and
right now all Angie kept thinking to herself was, if this girl's
marriage fails, then so be it, but she was not going to condone
her ever leaving her baby behind. Angie immediately wondered

if maybe this was what Jade needed. Maybe she needed to find happiness, real love, in order to be happy with herself and finally as a mother to a baby who needed her.

"I'm not going to tell you this is wrong, Jadey," Angie finally spoke. "Just be careful and smart. I was not at your age and being senseless cost me. But, honey, if this is what you need to come alive, grab ahold of it and coast."

Jade smiled at her. "Is that your shrink's way of telling me not to rush things?"

"You could say that," Angie replied, with a chuckle. "Now go home to your baby."

Chapter 5

Three nights went by with much of the same happening at Shooters after hours. Brock continued to show up shortly before closing time and Jade was dolling herself up a little more each night, anticipating his arrival. Their time together continued with endless conversation and increasing intensity as their physical attraction to each other was growing.

Jade was cleaning up the dishes on the table and counter top in her kitchen at lunchtime when the baby was down for a nap and Rhett unexpectedly came home.

"Hi," he said as he walked in their kitchen door from the outside and he caught the screen door before it slammed, to not wake the baby if she was asleep.

"Why are you home already?" Jade asked, feeling relieved she was doing something productive when he walked in. She didn't need to give him another reason to be angry with her.

"Lunch," he replied, opening the fridge and she watched him in his Spengler Plumbing uniform of blue jeans, brown work boots, and a red short-sleeved button down shirt with the S emblem and Spengler spelled out underneath it. His jeans sagged in the rear end and Jade caught herself thinking about the firm, tight end that Brock Green had in a pair of denim.

"There isn't much in there," Jade said referring to food in the refrigerator.

"Never is," Rhett responded as he shut the door and turned around. "We need to talk. We never have the chance to anymore because when I come home from work, you rush out to Shooters. Seems like lately you leave earlier and earlier and you're dressing sexier, too." Jade tried not to change her expression as she stood by the sink and allowed him to speak. She wondered if he had heard something. Maybe one of his co-workers had seen her talking to Brock, or worse. They had not kissed in the parking lot anymore. They were doing that inside of the empty bar now. Brock still didn't know Jade was married, or had anything to hide. She knew she would have to tell him eventually. She was just buying time right now, or just enjoying the moment.

"I bartend, Rhett. Sexy brings good tips," Jade told him matter-of-factly.

"Who's the guy?" he asked her outright.

"Who tips me?" she asked. "They all do," she added.

"The cowboy. The one I heard looks at you like he wants to put his hands all over you," Rhett's voice quivered as he looked at his wife and waited to hear the worst.

"Men get drunk in bars, you can't tell one from the other after awhile. They all have the same thing on their minds. I'm just working, Rhett. We need the money, you know that."

"What I know is that we don't act like we are in a marriage anymore, not sure if we ever did." He walked toward her and she didn't move. He got close to her face with his, really close and he attempted to press his lips to hers but she backed away. He pushed forward and planted a hard kiss on her. His mouth was open and his tongue brushed hard on hers. "I want you. Now." He put his hand up her shirt and she cringed.

"I can't. I'm on my period," she lied, and backed away from being so close to him.

"Remember the story about your Gramma?" Rhett asked his wife, who remained silent. "Her husband, Dane. People say he loved her with everything he had. He didn't want to lose her. I'm like Dane." And that was all he said before he walked through their kitchen and back out of the side door. This time he let it slam and a moment later Jade heard the baby cry.

"Damn you," Jade said aloud in her kitchen. And then she instantly made up her mind that tonight was the night she was going to go all the way with Brock Green. She didn't feel like a married woman anymore, and she certainly didn't like the hold Rhett believed he had over her. She didn't care if he loved her or how much he wanted her. And, she almost felt afraid of how he implied being in control of keeping her there.

***

Jade hired her teenage neighbor girl to watch the baby one hour before she expected Rhett home from work. She was dressed and ready, and she wanted to get out of the house before her husband came home. She didn't want him to pick up on the obvious change in her. She didn't want to have her husband on her mind at all. She was thinking about Brock Green and what could lie ahead with him. She wasn't someone who planned in advance or thought about the future, she lived in the moment and she sure was enjoying the stolen moments with this new man.

It was getting closer to closing time than usual and still no Brock. The bar was less crowded and Jade was feeling impatient. *What if he didn't show up? What if he was with another woman? What if he got hurt on the jobsite? How would she even know?* She was testy with the other customers tonight and just wanted her shift to end, and when it did she was sad and disappointed. *Maybe Gram was right,* she thought, *maybe I should have used more sense and not allowed myself to get so caught up in him, a stranger nonetheless.*

Jade flipped the switch to turn off the bar's open sign in the window and then she dimmed the lights in the room. When she walked toward the door to lock it, someone pushed it open from the other side.

He looked the same as always. Rugged and handsome and unbelievably sexy in his cowboy getup. He closed the door behind him quickly, and said, "I'm running late tonight, sorry. As the foreman of our project, I have hours of paperwork at the close of every work day. We ran into some problems today and I had a phone conference with my boss back home that went overtime." Jade was watching him speak, the way his mouth moved, his facial expressions, and the way his skin creased on his forehead. She was standing there in a tight, little black dress with black stilettos. She looked dressed for a fancy nightclub, rather than a down-home bar.

"I'm glad you're here now," she said, smiling at him with her eyes.

"You look amazing," he said, looking at all of her.

"Thank you," she said, stepping closer to him and he put his hands around her waist and then moved them onto her bottom. She smoothed her hands over his chest, over top of another starched, white shirt, and then she unbuttoned the first few buttons. She felt inside, his chest was tight and she bent her head down and kissed his left nipple. He responded by putting his hands on the back of her neck, encouraging her to do more. She proceeded to take his shirt entirely off and then they began kissing as they moved in sync and away from the window and over toward the bar. She reached for his belt buckle and undid it. And then the button fly on his jeans was completely undone.

This cowboy preferred commando and she let out a flirty giggle when she saw his manhood.

"You're stripping me in a bar," he said, his voice sounding hoarse.

"Yes, I am," Jade responded as she put her hands on him and he immediately hardened. He pulled her closely, gently but with an intense desire to be with her. He kissed her full on the mouth repeatedly as she kept her hand in his pants. She was still wearing her fitted black dress when he finally put his hands underneath it from the bottom and slipped it up and over her head. She was standing there in her black bra, matching thong and black stilettos. She moved his pants down to his calves, over his boots. He caressed her breasts through her bra and then quickly slipped it off her. He touched her, kissed her, devoured her, and drove her to the brink. He was sitting bare-assed on a bar stool when she swung her legs over him and he literally tore off her thong. She sat on him as he entered her immediately. She rocked over him, and ended up pouncing repeatedly until he lifted her up and off of him for a moment. He found her with two of his fingers and she throbbed, standing in front of him. She felt weak in the knees and came almost immediately and explosively before he set her back onto his lap and found pleasure in finishing what she had started, and wanted from the moment he walked into that bar room tonight.

***

She was in bed, trying to sleep next to her husband. All she could think about was being with another man just hours before. She had to tear herself away from Brock Green tonight, and he from her. He told her she was amazing and he knew his business trip there was for a reason. He was meant to meet her. He said he would return tomorrow night and she told him she would be there.

Jade never tossed and turned that night. She just laid there, still and staring up at the ceiling in the pitch dark bedroom. Rhett snored until his alarm sounded at four-fifteen and that's when Jade pretended to be asleep. After she heard him shower, get dressed, and then leave, she sat up in their bed and brought her knees to her chest. The white babydolls she was wearing made her feel sexy. She had not felt sexy in a very long time. It had nothing to do with the pajamas she was wearing, however, and everything to do with the affair she had just begun.

By the third consecutive night, the sex continued in the bar and their connection deepened. The conversations they shared, lying naked in each other's arms in the backroom of the bar on a worn brown leather sofa, were open and honest. At least Brock was being truthful. And Jade felt it was time he knew she was not just a single woman living in a small house on the north side of the city he was called to work in for six months.

"I have to tell you something, something I've withheld from you. I know why I didn't tell you. I didn't want to scare you off." Brock was listening as she laid on top of him and lifted her head up off of his chest to look him in the eyes. "I was not happy for a very long time, not until you came into my life,"

Jade paused. "I have a baby who is six months old and I've been stuck in an unhappy marriage for eight months." Jade wanted to add how it was a marriage and a family that she desperately wanted out of before, and now she really did, but she allowed him to process what she had just revealed.

He immediately tried to sit up with her still lying on top of him. She moved and so did he. He sat there for a moment before he spoke. "I am not a home wrecker."

"My home was wrecked long before you came into town," she tried to reassure him. "I was pregnant and I married a man I do not love. I have, so many times, wanted to just pack up and leave it all behind."

"But, your baby..." he said, feeling startled and confused.

"I can't help how I feel. She has a good father, but I'm not the mother for her. I want more out of life than being stuck there forever." Jade was being brutally honest and Brock allowed her to continue speaking. "I know you must think I'm some kind of freak now. Who doesn't love and bond with a baby, especially their own?" Jade was beginning to cry as she spoke. This was the first time she felt emotional about wanting to throw it all away. Never before had she allowed herself. It was the effect Brock had on her, she knew that.

"You're only human," he finally spoke to her. "We all deserve to be happy. Think it through, I mean thoroughly, because that would be some regret to wake up with one day and have to live with for the rest of your life. But, if you decide to leave, if you feel it in your heart that you need to get out of this town and leave your life as you know it, I will be the one behind the wheel of that own-the-road truck waiting at the end of your driveway."

The tears spilled over in her eyes and he pulled her naked body close to his again. "Be sure. You've got six months." She heard his words and she suddenly felt excited about the future. A future with him.

"Are you for real? I thought you'd be livid and storm out of here, never wanting to see me again," Jade admitted to him.

"What I feel is for real," he replied, "and what I feel for you is love."

She told him she loved him too, and she meant those words with all of her being. He kissed her softly after they professed their love for each other, and then he held her.

Chapter 6

Jade avoided her grandmother for one week, and then she couldn't take it anymore. She missed her, and she desperately wanted to confide in her.

When Jade walked into Angie's kitchen after she rang the doorbell once, she found her unpacking two bags of groceries on top of the table.

"Jadey, it's so good to see you," Angie said, pretending as if she didn't already sense that her granddaughter was, by now, involved with the cowboy she had already told her about.

"Good to see you, Gram." Jade kissed her on the cheek. She didn't feel guilty coming to her today, or ever, because she knew this woman. She knew Angie Roberts as more than just an elderly woman whom she called her grandmother. She saw her as a woman, a real woman who had survived the trials of life, and made her share of mistakes along the way.

"So tell me what's changed. Are things any different, better, at home? And, have you ridden that cowboy yet?" Jade howled with laughter and Angie did too. She had to keep this situation lighthearted. She remembered being the same way. She wanted men, a lot of men, in her day.

"Home life sucks, Rhett makes me miserable and I just go through the motions with Aspen. She's a good baby, thank God, because I'd lose my mind if she cried all the time." Angie again wished Jade had brought her along. She assumed the same babysitter was being hired regularly now. "And, yes, I'm sleeping with him. We love each other, Gram. It's for real, and it's going to last."

"Have you told him you're married with a baby?" Angie was worried about this affair. If this turned out not to be what Jade believed, she could foresee her hitting rock bottom. And Angie worried about her being stable enough to pick herself up and carry on if her hopes, and brand new dreams, were to be crushed.

"I didn't at first, but he knows now. He's supportive and he wants to be with me." Jade had excitement in her eyes and in her voice. Angie only wished she had met someone like Brock before she had gotten pregnant and married a man she didn't love. She knew though from the experience of having lived seventy-five years, difficult ones at times, how life never happened easily and conveniently.

Angie left her groceries and sat down at the table with Jade as she told her about Brock being a construction foreman, only in town for six months. When Jade told her of her plans to run away with him at the end of his job here, Angie put her hand over her mouth.

"If anything is going to kill me, it will be you leaving–"

"Gram, we will still talk, everyday, and I will teach you how to FaceTime and–"

"Let me finish," Angie said, sternly. "What will kill me is if you leave your baby. Don't do it, Jadey! Take her with you. She's yours. You know I've spent my entire life trying to make up for the hurt I caused when I made that same shameful choice." Angie had tears welling up in her eyes when Jade told her she was not planning to bring her baby along with her when she moved to Tennessee with Brock Green.

***

Only a day went by before Angie called Sher and asked her to come see her. It was summertime, but being a school principal, she still worked each day. Sher told her mother she would stop by after work. The more Angie thought about the repercussions of breaking Jade's confidence, the less she wanted to tell Sher the truth. Angie was torn and so she called her other daughter, Sadie. Sadie lived and worked in St. Louis. She, like her mother, felt drawn to that city and thrived in it. At fifty years old, her career as a psychiatrist was successful and still flourishing. Sadie made Angie proud in so many ways because of her kind heart, because of her forgiving nature, but most of all because she attained the dream Angie never reached. Sadie was married to an orthodontist named Lucas for thirty-three years and the two of them shared two sons, Brandon and Aaron, who were seventeen and nineteen years old.

Sadie arrived at Angie's house first. Angie smiled warmly at her when she walked in and immediately embraced her. She looked exactly like Angie, twenty-five years ago. Sadie could also have been mistaken as Jade's mother. The three of them shared the same body type, hair, and facial features. It was Sher who favored Dane and that too warmed Angie's heart. Dane was a handsome man, and a good man. She continued to feel sorry and saddened knowing his life was cut entirely too short. He was an amazing, exceptional, loving father to her girls and, for that, Angie felt a genuine love for him. She was never in love with him, but she loved the person he became when Angie struggled with her own identity and where she belonged. He never wavered in his strength and loyalty, and he loved his daughters unconditionally.

"You look good, mom," Sadie said, pulling out of her embrace and standing before her wearing fitted black pants, black chunky pumps, and a sleeveless fuchsia button down blouse. Angie looked trendy in her light-washed denim capris and a scoop neck lime green cotton shirt with flip flops to match. "Keep it up, whatever you're doing and confide in me how you do it, because I want to age just like you." Angie smiled at her, and replied, "Sex and booze, daily," and they both giggled.

After they shared small talk and caught up on each other's present happenings, Angie confided in Sadie about Jade. And when she told her sweet-natured daughter that Jade, too, was planning to leave her family, Sadie covered her mouth with her hand and began to cry. The pain was still there, maybe not raw anymore after consecutive decades, but it was present.

"Mom, she can't. Tell her she can't. You can explain how you felt and what it cost you." Sadie sounded as if she was begging her mother to do something, anything to stop another tragedy of the same from occurring. It was a cruel and unimaginative thought to fathom how history could repeat itself in the worst way.

"I've tried, and I can't seem to get through to her and it worries me as much as it does you, even moreso, how she is adamant about this," Angie said. "I know she is basing her decision on falling in love. That man is good to her, loves her, wants her, she says. I want my Jadey to feel a love like that. I want that for her."

"Because you never had it," Sadie said, feeling sad for her mother. She knew the sacrifices she made once she returned to their home. She watched her, year after year, and recognized the loneliness.

"I've done okay without it, baby girl," Angie said, softly smiling, "but having someone to love and be loved by is what makes life extra special."

Before the two of them could talk further, the door opened up and Sher walked in. She was wearing a cobalt blue skirt, just above her knees, with a black three-quarter-length-sleeved button down blouse, and black pointed-toe heels. She was talking loudly on her cell phone and continued to do so when she made eye contact with her twin sister first and smiled broadly. Sadie waved big at her sister, a sister she had always been very close to and loved so deeply, and then Sadie turned her back to Sher and looked directly at her mother. Her voice was low, but Angie heard her clearly. "Do not tell her. She will kill Jade. We will figure out something, just don't tell her. Not yet." Angie nodded her head in agreement. She knew she had asked Sadie there for a reason. She needed reassurance that she was doing the right thing for Jade, by keeping such a huge secret from her granddaughter's own mother.

A minute later, Sher was off of her phone and hugging her sister. Again, she refrained from sharing that kind of closeness with her mother. Her struggles with Jade had intensified the rift between them, especially in the last two years. Sher was at least two inches taller than Sadie, and thinner. Both of them were striking at age fifty. Aging gracefully was obviously in their genes, as Angie truly looked a decade younger than seventy-five.

"What brings you across the river, sis?" Sher asked Sadie as they separated but still remained standing close.

"Just checking on mom," she replied, making eye contact with Angie and wondering what kind of excuse her mother would fabricate now that they agreed not to tell Sher the truth.

"You okay? Is there a reason you called me, or the both of us, here?" Sher cared, and she loved, she just chose not to be too obvious about it when it came to her mother.

"I'm wonderful," Angie replied. "Do I need an excuse to bring both of my girls home at the same time? You know how I adore the bond you two have always had." Sadie smiled at Sher, hoping she was buying the story.

"It's only natural that we bonded, we were all each other had after daddy died and you repositioned yourself back into our lives." Sher could be cruel, and Sadie shook her head before speaking.

"Alright already, sis. Stop beating a dead horse. We're fifty years old for chrissakes." Sadie was trying, but Sher was in one of her moods to push.

"Fifty years old and one of you has yet to grow up," Angie said, always being good for adding fuel to Sher's fire.

"Oh, of course, I'm so immature. I run a school district, mother. I think I've got it together when it comes to adulthood."

"I'm very proud of you both, can we change the subject now?" Angie said, regretting her interjection.

"Yes. How's my daughter?" Sher asked, and Sadie's eyes widened.

"Doing well," Angie replied, trying to sound convincing. "She is really trying with Baby Aspen and she works so damn hard every night at Shooters."

"I've heard she flirts too much with that cowboy who's in town for several months, working construction at the Base," Sher said, obviously annoyed. "She had better be ending her shift and going home to her husband and baby."

"Some marriages do not work out," Angie said to Sher. "You know that as well as I do." Sher divorced her husband,

Larry Woll, when he confessed to being bisexual. He ended up remarrying, a man, and he too now lived in St. Louis. Sher was heartbroken, but would never admit to it. Her failed marriage and the loss of a man she truly loved only added to her bitterness about life.

"I was in it for the long haul, mother. It was Larry who preferred his partner to have skin between the legs. I couldn't help him with that." Sadie chuckled and Sher winked at her as Angie rolled her eyes. "Just keep me in the loop if you find out Jade is doing something crazy. I swear I will beat some sense into her if I have to." Angie and Sadie were now certain keeping Jade's predicament from Sher was the right decision.

"Apparently she senses how you'd rather beat her than talk to her, so she comes to me," Angie said, again pissing off her daughter.

"Oh fuck you, mother!" Sher blurted out, completely fed up, and Sadie scolded her with an immediate, "That is enough, Sher!" response. "Show some respect."

"Respect her?" Sher pointed at a woman who was not shaken by her daughter's hatred which often times flared up. Angie could hold her own. She defined strong. "She's the woman who abandoned her babies," Sher continued, "and then returned four years later, more for circumstances rather than need, or want, or a yearning to love and be with her children."

"This is old news," Angie said, raising her voice. "You know damn well I was, from that day forward, a very good mother to you and your sister."

"You had your moments, I guess," Sher responded, "but you never made popcorn!" The words coming from Sher sounded ridiculous, but the three of them instantly froze and momentarily stood in silence. Angie was not sure exactly what Sher meant, so she asked her. She didn't want to, but she did regardless.

"What does that mean? Why are you talking about popcorn?" Angie held her breath for her own personal, painful memory.

"The neighbor kids had a mom who always made popcorn for them, you know, the Meyers." Sher wanted to leave it at that now, but Sadie pushed her.

"No, Sher, tell her what you really meant." Sadie was adamant this time.

"We always had popcorn with daddy," Sher said, almost sounding like an innocent child again. "It was our time with him, we sat on the floor in the living room with the popcorn bowl in the middle of the three of us. We were little, as you know, but we knew how special that ritual was. It was our time at the end of every day with our daddy, with our little family of three." Sher sounded as if she choked on her words and Sadie had tears in her eyes. But, it was Angie who appeared most affected by the story. Her face was wet with tears as Sher continued on. "I asked you once, soon after daddy died and you moved in with us, if you would make popcorn. Your response was, no, you didn't like popcorn. I never asked you again, but I hated you for that, too."

Angie let out a whimper and began to sob. Both of her daughters were taken by surprise. They had never seen anything but a pillar of strength in the woman they called their mother. She never cried in front of them. Only once, they remembered seeing her break down when her own mother, their grandmother, died. Sadie was the first to reach for Angie, and Sher only watched her try to pull herself together.

"How strange it is to know that popcorn, of all things, has sentimental meaning to us all," Angie began, as Sadie handed her a tissue to dry her face. "My daddy used to say I made the best popcorn in the world. He asked me to pop some on the stovetop quite often. He was a good man like your daddy, and you both know he was lost to me when I was only nine." Angie paused to dab her eyes and blow her nose before she continued telling her story. " I remember the night so clearly, the night he died. It still pains me. And that is why I told you I didn't like popcorn," Angie looked at Sher. "My daddy said he would be right back, he had forgotten his wallet out in the garage, inside the glove box of his pickup truck. I told him to hurry because our popcorn was almost ready. I found him in the garage a short while later, slumped over in his truck. They said he had a heart attack. He wasn't even forty years old and he was lost to me. My life forever changed that night, so forgive me if I never wanted to see or smell or taste popcorn ever again." Angie shook her head and cleared her throat as Sadie felt terribly sorry for her and Sher felt guilt seep into her heart. "But, do know this, if I had known your daddy created a special memory like that for you girls, I would have put my pain aside and done the same. Maybe it would have helped me to heal. I certainly would have made the best damn popcorn this side of the Mississippi River. If I had known."

Chapter 7

Jade was watching her husband hold their baby girl on his lap. He had just returned home from work and immediately taken Aspen out of her swing in the living room. The baby's reaction to her daddy was priceless. There was an undeniable excitement in her eyes and on her little face as her limbs moved in sync at a rapid pace. Rhett could hardly keep her still on his lap as he spoke to her. He was laughing out loud and was obviously just as happy to see her. Jade should have felt guilty watching her baby react so happily. All day long, she did not act that lively, because Jade did not interact or play with or talk to her baby.

Jade was almost ready to walk out of the door to work the nightshift at Shooters. She was wearing her hair up in a loose bun, her makeup was flawless, and she had slipped into a short red skirt with her favorite button down white blouse. She didn't have much money to buy new clothes, but she had started wearing some dressier styles which she had hanging in her closet and never wore much. She used to slip on jeans and a Shooters tank top to work at the bar each night. Now, she was dressing for Brock Green.

They had been having an affair for six weeks. He continued to meet her at Shooters each night, just before closing time. There wasn't much the two of them had not talked about. They knew each other well now, their minds as well as their bodies. Jade knew every freckle, every blemish, every scar on that man's body. He was built flawlessly in Jade's eyes and if he had any imperfections, she didn't care.

As she was slipping into her black stilettos near their small kitchen table, Rhett called after her from the living room.

"You look beautiful again tonight, babe," he said, sincerely. "Do you think you can make it home earlier than three tonight? You know I don't sleep sound until you get home." Jade knew what he meant. He wanted to be intimate. Their baby was now eight months old and it had been six months since they had sex. Jade previously used the excuse of not completely being healed from giving birth. Rhett had not known any better, and she just did not want him. And after she met Brock Green, there was no turning back for her. She never wanted to be with any other man. He was it for her. Jade wondered how much longer she would be able to make excuses, or how much patience Rhett had. She just wanted the months to pass quickly so she could run away with the man she loved. Leaving it all behind was still exactly what Jade believed she wanted.

"I will try," she answered, "but you know there's always work to do after I close." Rhett had never asked her again about the cowboy he heard had frequented the bar and paid special attention to his wife. Jade assumed the townspeople had stopped talking. They were trying to be less flirtatious while there were people in the bar, and several times Jade had followed him back to his hotel room for a few hours. It felt more romantic to be with him in a bed, rather than on a couch in the back room of a bar.

"See what you can do," Rhett said, walking into the kitchen with the baby in his arms and he tried to kiss his wife goodbye. She leaned forward and gave him a peck on the cheek, and ignored their baby cooing in his arms. And then she walked out the door.

***

Jade slipped out of her stilettos in the dark kitchen as soon as she entered the house. She didn't want the noise from her hard shoes to wake up Rhett before his alarm sounded in less than an hour. It was three-thirty in the morning and she had just come from Brock's hotel room. She was tired, but running on adrenaline. Being in love wired her every night, and during the day when she was home alone with the baby, she napped more than she should have, even when the baby was awake.

She carried her shoes, from the inside heel with two fingers, as she walked barefoot down the short hallway to the bedroom she shared with her husband. She had her wrinkled, short, red skirt and white blouse back on, but her hair was loose and hanging down now. The bun had come out when she and Brock were in bed together again.

When she turned into the doorway of the bedroom, she expected to see Rhett lying underneath the covers on the bed, on his back with his hands up over his head. That is how he always slept, especially when he was sleeping sound. Before she even glanced at the bed, she gasped out loud when she saw him sitting in the armchair beside their bed. She looked for the baby in his arms, assuming first that she may have kept him awake again. Aspen wasn't there. It was just Rhett, dressed in a white, short-sleeved crewneck undershirt and gray-plaid boxer shorts. "You scared me!" Jade said, trying to keep her voice low.

"Sorry. I couldn't sleep. I was waiting for my wife to come home. Again." Rhett's voice sounded strange and he only stared straight ahead in the dark room. Jade walked over to the closet and cracked the door and turned on the light inside of it. She felt shaken, finding Rhett awake and waiting for her, and the dark room suddenly added to her fear.

"I wish you wouldn't count on me early each night," she said. "Once I close, I have too much work to do."

"I haven't seen any extra money coming in to compensate for your long hours," Rhett said, matter-of-factly and Jade ignored him.

"I'm going to take a shower," she said, walking toward the door of their bedroom and he immediately stood up from his chair and he took quick steps to get in front of her and keep her in the room.

"I'm not going to ask you who he is," he spoke to her and she tried to appear nonchalant with him, "I'm just going to assume he's someone you will get over."

"I don't know what–" she started to speak, she was ready to once again deny having an affair, but Rhett abruptly interrupted her.

"Because if you don't, I will kill him."

He stepped aside for his wife to leave. She was allowed to leave the room, but in his mind she was not allowed to leave him. He had heard all of the gossip about his wife and that cowboy. He was hurt and he was angry, but more than anything he was adamant about holding on to what was his. Even if he had to take drastic measures.

Chapter 8

"Gram, I was actually scared of him." Rhett was at work, the baby was again being cared for by the teenage neighbor, and Angie was at home, sitting at her kitchen table with Jade.

"Did he threaten you?" Angie asked her granddaughter.

"No. I don't think he would hurt me, but I never thought he had it in him to say he would kill somebody." The fear that escalated inside of Jade when she thought Brock's life could be in danger was unreal. The thought of losing Brock was far worse for her than the idea of something happening to her.

"Now, Jadey, I think we've all said that out of context before. Do you know how many times your mother has expressed how she could kill me?" Angie chuckled, and Jade wanted to believe her. There was just something about the way Rhett spoke. His eyes looked as if he meant every syllable of those threatening words.

"I have to get out of there. I can't wait any longer," Jade told her grandmother.

"Then pack up the baby and leave him, but don't you dare leave that baby. Jadey, you aren't still planning to abandon her, are you?"

Jade's eyes were fixated on the table top in front of her. There were four, checkered, red and white cloth placemats with frayed ends and Jade was touching the threads on the one in front of her with the tips of her fingers. Then, she looked over at her grandmother. There were no tears in her eyes and no hesitation in her voice. "She's far better off without me, Gram. Please, don't try to tell me otherwise."

"I'm running out of words for how to do that," Angie replied. "Any attempt I've made to get through to you, to make you see how dire of a mistake that would be, has not sunken into that beautiful, hard head of yours. I've been there, sweetie. I felt nothing." Then, Angie got up from her chair at the kitchen table and walked away. She was rummaging through a drawer in the living room and Jade waited for her to return. When she did come back, she was carrying a photograph in her hand. "See this, Jadey," Angie said, sitting down beside her again and placing the photograph on the table. Jade saw a black and white Polaroid of two babies. She knew one was her mother and the other her aunt. "I spent the first year of their lives with them, but I don't remember this. I never took a single picture of them. They were my babies and I couldn't have cared less. Then, five years later when I did care and I did love, they weren't babies anymore. They were children who knew exactly what I did and why. Sadie, as always, was more forgiving, but Sher still has her moments of hating me and she's a half of a century old."

Jade stopped looking at the photograph and bore her eyes into her grandmother's. She was wise, so wise, Jade believed. Yet, Jade could not seem to make herself hear her. It was as if she had to make her own mistakes in order to understand.

"When I look at them, as babies in this picture, I see glimpses of the future. In their eyes, they still look exactly the same now. Our identities are with us from the very beginning," Angie tried to explain. "Not just facial features, but who we are." She paused before continuing. "And, how we are treated molds us as people. Begin to love Aspen, learn to love her or she will be that little girl sitting in the school classroom looking around her and she will feel different. I will never forget a time right after I moved in with my girls. Dane had just died, and there was so much pain in that house. I stood outside of my girls' bedroom when I had been walking down the hallway and overheard them talking. Sadie was telling Sher to *look on the bright side, we now have a mom for when the teacher says make something special for your mom for Mother's Day.* And then Sher interjected, *but now we don't have a dad for those special days like Father's Day and just every day. He made every day special and I would much rather have him here than her. She's not our mother. She didn't love us, so she doesn't deserve our love.*"

Jade's eyes widened, "Even then, mom could be cruel."

"Maybe so," Angie said, "but she spoke the truth."

"So you're telling me, once again, that I will regret walking away someday and Aspen will hate me for it. Gram, don't you think I've thought about that? I understand, but I honestly believe she will be better off without me. If she grows up hating my memory, then so be it. That is far better than if she grows up hating me because she sees and feels how much I hate my life. I don't want to be there anymore. I'm starting over, starting fresh with Brock Green. He makes me happy, he fulfills me in ways I've never imagined."

"So, the sex is good," Angie interrupted. "That doesn't last."

"It's not just that, Gram. He gets me. He accepts me, faults and all, and at the same time he makes me want to be a better person. Do you think I want to tend bar for the rest of my life? I'd like to make something of myself, just like you did when you were away, Gram." Jade reached for Angie's hand on the table, and it was shaking. Her hands were lined and wrinkled on her fingers and around the knuckles. The hands of a strong woman who dealt with loss, decisions, and pain, and she survived. She thrived at times. And Jade knew she would as well. "It's okay, I will be okay. I promise."

As they sat at the table talking, Angie's nineteen-inch flat screen television placed on her kitchen countertop was on. The noon news was broadcasting live and a reporter was on the scene of an accident at Scott Air Force Base. It took Jade a moment to focus her attention on what the news was reporting.

"Turn it up, Gram!" It sounded as if something happened at the Base.

The two of them listened to seasoned reporter Robin Smith as they both stood directly in front of the screen. Jade put both of her hands over her mouth when she heard there was an accident fifty-seven minutes ago at a new construction site on the Base. Details were still emerging, but there was one fatality reported. Jade hurried to turn up the volume again, as if increasing the sound would bring more information from the news. The live broadcast then cut to a commercial and Jade just stood there.

"It could be him, Gram." Jade had never cared like this about anyone. The thought of losing him terrified her.

"You don't know that, Jadey," Angie tried to reassure her. "There could be more than one construction site there."

Jade didn't respond as the news resumed from the commercial break and the anchor in the studio reiterated that KMOV News 4 was the first on the scene at Scott Air Force Base in O'Fallon, Illinois, where a construction foreman lost his life in an accident.

"No!" Jade cried out, and Angie already knew Brock Green was a foreman. "I have to go there! Let me take your car!" Before Jade could run out of there, she needed her grandmother's car keys, but Angie did not budge.

"You will not get past the gate without military identification. You have no reason or connection to be on the premises," Angie reminded her. "Wait to hear. This may not even be what you're thinking right now."

"I have to try, Gram! Please...your keys?"

Angie walked over to the counter and found her car keys. Jade grabbed them from her and ran out of the door. She backed her grandmother's compact white Lincoln MKZ out of the detached garage and sped off. She raced down Smiley Street, ignoring yield signs and only yielding at stop signs. She finally made a left turn onto Route 50. She moved steadily through three stop lights, two greens and one yellow, and then she made a right turn onto Scott-Troy Road. Scott Air Force Base was just three miles ahead.

There was a line of cars at the gate. Jade was about to lose her mind waiting...and wondering if Brock was alive. She didn't pray much, in fact she could not remember the last time she asked God for anything. But, she was desperate now. She would have gotten on her knees at this moment if she could have. Instead, she just spoke aloud in the car. "Please, God, please. I can't lose him. I know you brought him into my life for a reason. Don't take him from me already." Jade wanted to give in to the tears welling up in her eyes and the quiver on her lips as she prayed, but she didn't. She was next in line at the gate and she had to hold it together.

She had no identification on her except for her driver's license. She watched the driver of the car in front of her show a badge of some sort. Employees were allowed through. Military personnel were waved on. Veterans were approved to enter. She was none of those and at this point she had no idea what she was going to say or do in order to get through that gate and find the construction site where Brock was working.

She pressed her foot gently on the gas pedal and then on the brake as she came to a stop near the guard. She took one look at the guard and breathed a sigh of relief. If there was one thing she was thankful for after having been born and raised in a close community, it was the fact that everyone knew most of the people around them. Roger Freeze looked very soldier-like, he even had the straight-faced expression until he recognized Jade. The two of them were close in high school. He hated math and Jade always allowed him to copy all of her answers, for homework and during tests. They were never caught, and they felt like quite a duo getting by with it, time and again. Roger Freeze always said he owed her, and now almost a decade later, it was payback time.

"Jade Woll... I'll be damned, still as beautiful as ever," Roger said, trying to conceal how happy he was to see her after all these years. He was a guard, paying his dues at that gate, and he was required to remain professional at all times.

"Thank you," Jade flashed a smile at him. "Listen, Rodge, I have nothing. No ID. You are going to be my free pass through here. I have to get to the construction site. Someone I love could have been hurt," she didn't want to say *or worse*, so she refrained.

"Jade, no, that could cost me my job," he said, sternly.

"You owe me, you cheater you," she smiled, but she felt impatient. She had to get through there.

"I do owe you, but not like this." As he spoke, Jade gave the car some gas and entered the Base grounds. She knew Roger Freeze would let her go. She, after all, saved his ass from failing math in high school.

She had no idea where she was headed, she just followed a few other cars, winding around the grounds and then she saw the excitement. Police cars, an ambulance with no lights or sirens on, and television news vans. She whipped the car off to the side of the road, parking behind the KSDK Channel 5 news van. She got out and was standing in the grass off to the side of the road wearing cut-off white denim shorts, a sleeveless pink plaid button down shirt, and white flip flops on her feet. She walked in the grass until she reached police tape, blocking off the path. She saw a building under construction about a hundred yards away. She saw the O'Fallon Chief of Police, Eric VanHook, being interviewed by a reporter, live, with the camera positioned directly on him. She stopped to listen to him answering one question after another. *Do you have a name of the man who fell victim to this tragic accident today?* Jade braced herself. She would not hear the name Brock Green. Even if that man, an officer of the law whom she knew and trusted, uttered his name, she would not allow herself to hear it. Her heart was not strong enough to love a man with everything she had...and then have to say goodbye. *Until the family is notified, we will not be releasing any further details.*

Jade felt on the edge. Her heart was about to beat out of her chest. The interview continued and she stayed out of the camera's way and walked off, remaining behind the police tape. And that's when she saw the hard hats. There were five or six men in white hard hats. They were the construction workers. She never thought twice, she just ducked under the police tape and ran. Someone hollered at her for crossing the police line, and that's when she saw the back of a man, standing in the middle of the construction crew. She ran, she kept running as fast as her legs would carry her. She saw him and she was not turning back or slowing down now. She could easily spot him in any crowd, anywhere. Broad shoulders, thick build, a tight end in a pair of denim that would make anyone look twice. He was hers and he was alive.

He had turned around and saw her, and stepped quickly toward her. When they reached each other, she fell into his arms and broke down. He held her. He knew she had thought it was him. It was a mistake made by the news media. The man who fell off of the scaffolding, through three floors to his death was not a foreman. He was a young, twenty-one-year-old boy, new to the crew this summer. Brock thought the world and all of that kid who originated from Franklin, Tennessee, just as he had.

"It's okay, shh..." Brock tried to calm her in his arms. "I know, I know. I'm fine though. You're not getting rid of me that easily, beautiful girl."

He couldn't spend much time with her, he said he was dealing with the police and the media and still trying to contact the victim's family three hundred miles away. She clung to him a little while longer and then he told her he would see her soon. Probably not tonight, but tomorrow for sure.

"I don't want to waste anymore time," Jade said to him, quickly. "I want to be with you. I can't wait months." Brock knew their project would now be delayed for investigation purposes. Returning to Tennessee at the end of a six-month projected deadline for completion was unlikely. "I'm leaving today, moving into your hotel room, if you'll have me."

"Jade, think this through. Call me later. You know I want you with me, the sooner the better, but calm down and think about this." He was holding both of her hands in his and then he let go as he stepped backward and then toward his crew. They were calling him back, they needed their foreman.

Chapter 9

Jade drove back to her grandmother's house. She had not changed her mind. If anything, she was even surer now than she was before. There was no time to waste. Life was precious and fragile and so unpredictable. She was given a second chance today. In an instant it could have all been over. Brock Green could have died at the construction site and Jade would have been left alone and miserable. That was how she saw her life. She had a husband whom she did not love. She had a baby whom she did not feel the slightest connection with. She wanted out, and she was determined to seize her freedom.

Angie met Jade outside as she was parking the car on the driveway. Jade had called her from her cell phone as soon as she left the Base grounds. She told her about the media's error. The foreman, her man, was alive and unharmed. Jade waited until she saw her grandmother in person to tell her what she was planning to do. Today.

"You can't, Jadey," Angie said to her, standing outside in the yard near the swing. They had been walking arm-in-arm toward the side door of the house, leading into the kitchen, when Angie stopped her granddaughter. "Do not make a rash decision based on relief from a dreadful experience."

***

Less than a half an hour later, Angie was dropping off Jade at her house. She didn't want her to walk home, especially in her frame of mind. When she pulled her car onto the rock driveway, Jade reached for the door handle on the passenger side. "Thanks, Gram. I love you."

"Call me, Jadey. Don't make me worry about you anymore than I already do." Angie felt the tears welling up in her eyes as she watched her granddaughter, a clone of herself fifty years ago, walk into her home. A home that probably would not be hers for much longer.

Angie never paid any attention in her rearview mirror to the truck that was pulling into the driveway after she had backed up and began to drive off. Rhett was home from work early to see his wife.

Jade was paying the babysitter when he walked in, and when the young girl left, Rhett spoke to his wife.

"Quite a day today, huh?" he asked her.

"I'm sorry, what do you mean?" she replied, wondering why he was home from work early and feeling miffed that she could not race through the house packing her things to ready for her escape after her shift at Shooters tonight. She wasn't going to go far, just to the hotel which sat through the field off of Interstate 64.

"I never get the chance to tell you much about how my work is going. You're not here to ask," Rhett began. "For weeks, we've been redoing the plumbing in an office building on Base." His words caught Jade's attention. The baby began to cry from her swing in the living room. She only wanted someone's attention. Even Rhett ignored her this time as he continued speaking. "A man lost his life today at a construction site."

"I did hear that on the news," Jade remained calm.

"Do you always rush out to accident scenes after you see a report on the news?" Jade's eyes widened. He stood in the middle of the living room floor, in his jeans and red uniform shirt with his work boots still on his feet. "You know what they say, no matter where you are or what you're doing, someone is always watching."

"Fuck you, Rhett!" Jade blurted out. "If you have something to say to me, just say it!"

"I saw you!" he screamed at her. "I saw you run to your lover. You looked scared out of your mind one minute and bursting at the seams with relief the next. Just think, it could have been him. You could have been lover-less and stuck with only the dream of being married to me for the rest of your life."

"I want out. I'm done, and I'm leaving. There is nothing left for me here." Jade's words were strong and fearless, until Rhett took two steps toward her and grabbed her by the shoulders. He was hurting her, and she winced. She tried to pull away from his grip, but that only made him strengthen his hold on her.

"You aren't going anywhere. Call your boss and tell him you will not be in to work tonight. We will be spending time together as a family, for once."

Jade lifted her knee up. She'd never done it before. She had seen it in happen firsthand when a fight broke out in the bar one night between a drunk man and his girlfriend. She remembered seeing that ticked-off girlfriend knee him right between the legs. The blow caused him to double over. And the same just happened to Rhett Connors.

Jade didn't look back. She wanted no part of him, their baby, or even their truck. She was going to run, literally. She didn't care about her clothes or her other belongings. She only wanted her freedom from this man, and the life as she had grown to despise.

She reached the door just as Rhett was back on his feet. She flung it open and found herself staring face to face with her grandmother. Rhett was then behind her, and Angie stepped up into the house, pushing them both further back inside.

She closed the door behind her, and stared at the man she now knew was capable of hurting her granddaughter. "Oh for chrissakes!" Rhett spoke, disrespectfully. "Gramma is here to save the day? Get the hell out, Ang!"

"Go pack your things, and I will take you away from here," Angie instructed Jade, but Jade was afraid to move. She feared what her husband might do to the one person she loved most in this world.

"Gram, no, you should go," Jade said, wanting to keep her out of harm's way.

"She's not going anywhere with you, or with her lover. She's mine, for better or for worse. Like it or not." Rhett spat the words at them.

Angie stood there calmly and smiled through clenched teeth. "You know, Rhett, I've been alone, without a husband or a partner for most of my entire life. I am a woman who knows how to protect herself." Rhett frowned at her, until she revealed the small handgun from her jean jacket pocket. It was one she had kept in her car's glove box. "I've never had to use it, so it might be worth a shot to say I did, just once. Pun intended."

Jade's eyes were as wide as Rhett's. "Now go pack your things, Jadey, while I keep this piss poor excuse of a husband company."

When Rhett backed off, he sat down on the sofa and Jade fled from the room. She threw everything from inside of her closet and her dresser drawers into two suitcases. She also dumped two drawers from the bathroom vanity into her suitcase, directly on top of her clothing. Makeup. Toiletries.

And, a Band-Aid box with a rolled up stash of cash from tips from the bar.

She returned to the living room only minutes later. Angie was still standing near the door, gun in hand. Rhett had not moved from the sofa, and the baby was still in the swing. Angie wanted to go over and pick her up, but she didn't. It wasn't her place to do so right now.

"I'm ready, Gram," Jade said as she carried both suitcases and didn't look over again at Rhett, or the baby.

"Get the baby," Angie said to her.

"What? No. I can't. I won't," Jade replied, and Rhett's attention peaked.

"She stays with me!" he spoke outright.

"Get your baby, Jadey. The two of you will be staying at my house for awhile." Angie was adamant. "You will be allowed to see her," she said to Rhett. "Those details will be worked out later." Rhett seemed satisfied for the moment, or maybe he was still scared of the gun in the old lady's hand.

"Gram, I will stay with you, if that is what you want, but–"

"The baby comes with us, or I leave you here, too." Angie did not mean those words. She never would have left her there, but she hoped Jade would believe her and want to leave badly enough, even if it meant changing her plans and bringing her baby along.

Jade stormed through the living room, bitching under her breath. It could have been a comical scene, but really it was just sad. What woman would not lay down her life for her own child? Angie had been there, in her exact frame of mind, and no one forced her to take her babies with her. Angie was doing all she could to write this story, the way it should read, for her granddaughter and her great-grandchild.

The baby seemed relieved to finally be freed from that swing and Angie tucked the gun safely into her jacket pocket as Jade and the baby approached her at the front door. Only she knew the gun was not loaded. Angie reached for Aspen and took her from Jade. "Go get her diaper bag and some of her things." Jade obliged, but she didn't pack much. Just enough for a day or two. She still, despite her grandmother's dire efforts, was not planning to keep her baby. For now though, she was grateful to have a safe place to flee.

Chapter 10

It didn't take long for Sher to discover that Jade and her baby were living with Angie. When she heard the news at school, secondhand from her secretary, Sher showed up at her mother's house.

Jade was in the living room, picking up a blanket and a few toys off of the floor. She actually had been making an effort to tidy up out of respect for her grandmother. She hoped they would not have to impose on her for much longer. She was ready to be with Brock, permanently. She had seen very little of him the past three days. He was working late nights and she agreed to return to her grandmother's house immediately after closing time each night. Leaving the baby in her care all night long was too much, Jade realized, but she was tired of the responsibility.

Sher didn't knock, she just let herself inside of her mother's house. When she stepped her heels onto the rug by the door, she saw Jade. "So, there's nothing quite like the humiliation of hearing your daughter has left her husband and moved in with her grandma." Sher was miffed, but grateful Jade had not left the baby, too.

"You should be used to how I've always been a disgrace," Jade replied. It was lunchtime and she wanted to go into the kitchen to prepare something to eat while the baby was napping. Angie had gone out to buy additional flowers for her backyard garden.

Sher remained standing by the front door. She was wearing a burnt orange linen skirt, which reached just above the knee, with a white camisole underneath the same burnt orange light sweater with three-quarter-length sleeves. Jade looked at her mother, towering her in nude heels. She was a woman who demanded attention and flaunted her power. Jade never felt close to her, and she believed she never would.

"I understand that marriages fail," Sher said, trying to show some compassion. "Is this just a temporary separation or do you want to divorce Rhett? Whichever the case, keep things amicable between the two of you, for Aspen's sake."

"I am the one who wants out, and Rhett let his anger get the better of him. I suppose he has every right to be irate. I'm having an affair, mom. I'm happier than I've ever been in my life," Jade explained, while Sher inhaled just enough air through her nostrils to keep herself quiet and calm. "Rhett and I have talked since things got out of hand, and a little physical between us. I think he understands now. I think he sees how unhappy we both were together."

"Did he hit you?" Sher asked, feeling compassion surface in her heart.

"No, but when he tried to manhandle me, I kneed him in the balls so hard that it didn't take but a second for him to realize I will not be pushed around or forced to stay with him."

"That's my girl," Sher said, offering a crooked smile, and Jade returned a genuine smile to her. Her mother rarely claimed her. "So the two of you are sharing Aspen while you work out some sort of custody arrangement?"

"Right now, he comes to visit her when I'm working my shift at Shooters," Jade answered. "Gram is here while he spends some time with Aspen. Last night, he took her home for a few hours and then brought her back. He's a good father, I don't have any doubt that my baby will be just fine with him."

"Meaning you plan to give him full custody?" Sher frowned. This was what she was afraid of. She knew her daughter all too well. She was irresponsible and self-centered and Sher's greatest fear was believing Jade had it in her to walk away, just like her own grandmother did.

"Yes, because I'm moving to Tennessee in just a matter of months," Jade replied, holding her own in front of her mother.

"With the cowboy you're screwing?" Sher's voice was calm, but her words were critical.

"With the man I love," Jade said, confidently.

"And he doesn't want to be tied down with your baby?" Sher asked.

"That's not it at all. It's me. I think you've seen it all along, mom. I'm the one who doesn't want to be a mother. I feel nothing for her. She does not deserve that," Jade heard her own voice crack and then she cleared her throat. "I'm walking away now because it's the way that will hurt the least, for her especially. She's too little to remember me."

"So get out while the going's good, huh?" Sher asked, feeling her insides tremble. She could not fathom abandonment. She never understood her own mother's actions when she was a child, and still as a grown woman.

Jade didn't answer her mother. She just stood there, hoping her visit would be short-lived. It was obvious she had taken a break from work to come there. Neither one of them were speaking momentarily. They didn't understand each other. They never had. Sher didn't mean for it to happen, but before she knew it, she had started to cry.

"Mom…" Jade said, not knowing what else to say at the moment. She was not accustomed to seeing her mother be anything but strong, sometimes to the point of being unfeeling.

Sher immediately wiped away the tears on her cheeks with her fingers. "Guess I'm showing how I really feel," she said softly. "You know, of all the things you've said to me today, one is resurfacing in my mind right now. You said, you're walking away now because it will hurt the least for Aspen. You think because she is a baby she doesn't know you're her mother? And, in turn, you think she will not realize you've left her? Take it from me, she will know. From as far back as I can remember, I knew. I felt empty. I felt lost. I felt undeserving." Jade only stared at her mother as she spoke and more tears fell. And finally, Sher said quietly, "Aspen will miss you, and so will I."

Jade tried to smile, but it just didn't seem appropriate to look or feel happy at this moment. "I'll miss you, too, mom," was all she said. Jade never added how she, too, will miss Aspen. Because she knew she wouldn't.

When Sher left, Jade felt spent. She was tired of the deep conversations with both her grandmother and now her mother. She knew they both, in their own way, were desperately trying to change her mind about leaving. And they had every right to make an attempt to stop her from making the biggest mistake of her life. That's the way everyone would see it. Family. Friends. Neighbors. Even strangers. It didn't matter though, because deep in her soul, Jade wanted to leave.

***

While her grandmother was still out flower shopping, Jade texted Rhett, telling him he could pick up Aspen again tonight and take her back home with him. She also offered for him to keep her all night long, if he wanted to. Jade didn't want her grandmother to lose any sleep because of the baby, and she was not planning to come back there after her shift was over. She had already made plans to see Brock after closing time, and what he didn't know yet was tonight was the night she was going to leave. She planned to move into his hotel room until the two of them could leave town together.

As she was packing her two suitcases again, Jade received a reply to the text she had sent to Rhett. All it said was "ok" and she was relieved he had come through for her, again. That only confirmed to her what she already knew. Rhett was a good father.

A few hours later, Angie was outside working in her garden when Jade was inside getting ready for work. She dressed up again in a short, fitted cobalt blue dress and black wedges. This was going to be a special night for her and Brock. She had planned to ask him to drive her back to her grandmother's house after midnight so she could get her suitcases from the outside cellar. She had already hidden them down there while Angie was gone.

Jade had thought of everything. She didn't want to risk waking her grandmother, startling her, or having another conversation where she would try to convince her to stay, and not to leave her baby.

From the kitchen window inside of the house, Jade saw Rhett pull up on the driveway. She had the diaper bag packed and the baby ready. Rhett was going to take her to Shooters on his way home with Aspen.

Jade pushed any second thoughts or jitters out of her mind. This was becoming all too real. She needed to stay focused and she was. And then she realized how she had not said goodbye to Aspen. She was sitting on the floor in the living room, playing with a caterpillar toy that spelled out the ABC's on its legs. It was musical and Aspen was mesmerized by it when Jade walked in. She knew Rhett would not get out of the truck, and would be waiting for her and the baby to come outside. Her few minutes to say goodbye would be now or never.

Her baby, at eight months old, was strong enough to pull herself up onto furniture, but she had not started to crawl yet. Jade knew this was because she had kept her restrained in a bouncy seat or swing during the day, sometimes all day long. Jade just did not want to be bothered with her baby, let alone try to meet her needs so she could grow and learn in a timelier manner.

She was out of time now. This was it. It was her choice to leave. She made her way down to the floor, on her knees because her dress was tight. Aspen, who was wearing a little pink sundress with only a diaper underneath and no shoes on her tiny bare feet, reached out for her. Jade remained kneeling on the carpeted area rug in the middle of the living room floor and her baby girl pulled herself up, by holding hands with her mommy's. Those little hands were clenching tight to Jade's fingers. Those tiny balled up fists were holding on for dear life, counting on her mommy. Jade was there. She helped her child balance, and then she looked into her eyes. She saw love. She saw trust. Complete trust. *Hold me up, mommy. Don't ever let me go. Help me. Love me.* Aspen was smiling and Jade could see all four of her teeth, two on top and two on bottom.

Jade batted her eyes to clear the tears welling up in them. She wasn't supposed to feel. Now was not the time. She had plans. She had dreams. And she couldn't achieve any of them with a baby being a burden to her.

She pulled Aspen close to her chest and kissed her on top of her head. She momentarily breathed in her scent. *Had she ever done that before?* Jade rose to her feet, with her daughter on her hip, and she walked outside to get into Rhett's pickup truck.

She placed Aspen into the car seat in the cramped backseat of the truck. She buckled her and found herself staring. Endlessly. Almost as if she was seeing her for the first time. When, really, it was the last.

Her baby was cooing and chewing on her fists. Drool was all over the place, on both hands, running on her arms to her elbows, and onto the material of the seatbelt.

"You okay?" Rhett asked her as he turned around from the driver's seat to the look into the backseat. She seemed different to him, and he had no idea why. He didn't have the slightest clue why she was not alright. She was beginning to feel something, and it saddened her and angered her simultaneously, because now it was too late.

"I will be," Jade answered.

Chapter 11

There wasn't a steady crowd at Shooters, and because she wasn't continuously busy, Jade was thinking too much. She felt teary and the lump in her throat, no matter how many times she swallowed, would not subside. The worst part of the night was when one of her regular customers, a man old enough to be her grandfather, asked how her baby was doing. *Getting big, I'll bet*, he said, and Jade couldn't speak. She only nodded her head and tried to smile before she looked away.

Whatever was happening to her, the feeling overwhelming her tonight, would dissipate. She told herself so, repeatedly. *It's just your nerves. You can't turn back now. Think of Brock and the future, the happily ever after you want with him.*

It was near closing time and Jade stood behind the bar, and poured herself a shot of whiskey. She tipped it back swiftly when her last two customers bid her a goodnight and walked out of the door. It burned going down, but whiskey was what she needed. She wanted her judgment clouded. She wanted her thought process to not make sense. Ever since she knelt down on the living room floor in front of her baby, something changed and she had begun to think differently. She couldn't go there. Not now. Not ever again. Jade poured, and drank, another shot of whiskey. This one made her eyes burn.

By the time she drank four shots, she had her wedges off because she had been stumbling around in them as she tried to clean up the bar room. She had forgotten to turn off the outside open sign still lit in the window and she had not remembered to lock the door. Brock expected to knock when he made his way up to the door outside, but instead he found it unlocked. And when he walked into the bar, he knew something was wrong.

"Hey there, what's going on?" he creased his brow and gave her a lopsided grin. She was wearing her tight, cobalt blue dress and her feet were bare.

"I'm just, just really, really, happy, um happy, to see you, my sexy, oh yes you are, cowboy," She was not slurring her words but repeating them and Brock giggled as she walked directly up to him, put her hands on his chest and kissed him full on the mouth. He responded, and then he spoke.

"Somebody tastes like whiskey tonight," he said, and she giggled.

"I may have had one, or four, shots after closing time," she admitted and his eyes widened.

"Holy Christ, you're drunk little lady," Brock said, wondering if there was a reason she had been drinking too much tonight. It wasn't like her to have one too many. She was around alcohol so much, she often times didn't even want any of it by the end of the night.

"Not drunk, just tipsy," Jade said, trying to keep her balance as she backed up a step.

"Why don't you sit," he offered, and pulled out a chair from under the nearest table. "I will finish up for you here and then drive you home." He knew she needed a ride anyway, because she was without a vehicle and Angie had been bringing her to work lately.

"Home is not where I'm going tonight," she said to him.

"Well I meant your Gram's house." She liked the way he called her grandmother, *Gram*, as she did.

"Not there either," she replied. "I have my suitcases packed and hidden in the cellar. I'm running tonight. I'm leaving. I know we can't leave town until your work is done here, but I'll call *home* the hotel room with you until we can get the hell out of dodge." Brock was looking at her, really looking, and he wondered just how certain she was about this. She appeared completely unsettled. Being drunk spoke volumes.

"So that explains your state of mind tonight," he said, reaching for her hand on the table top. "Regret will eat at your soul, Jade. Be sure about this."

The tears, the ones welling up in her eyes all evening, finally broke loose. She wanted to say she was sure, she was damn sure. She had waited months, eight to be exact, to do this. She was not going to soften now. Changing her mind was not an option. "I am sure," she replied, wiping her tears. "I just feel emotional, I'm sorry."

Brock leaned forward and kissed her on the forehead. He placed both of his hands on each side of her face and he looked her directly in the eyes. "Let me take you back to your Gram's. I will get those suitcases out of the cellar and tuck you into your bed there. Sleep on this. Sleep off the whiskey," he giggled a little, "and worry about making life-changing decisions in the morning, or days or weeks from now."

"No!" she said, abruptly. "That's not what I want. Not what I need. Please. No. Just take me with you." She sounded almost childlike. Wounded and desperate. And Brock was not sure what he was going to do to be able to help her. They had never talked about the possibility of having her baby in tow when they exit onto Interstate 64 to drive out of town, en route to Tennessee and their new life together. He wasn't sure what to say, or what to think, now. He knew he loved her, but he honestly wondered now if that would be enough. "Say something," she added, worried he changed his mind. She was angry at herself again. Angry for feeling so vulnerable and she forced herself, right then and there, to believe this self-doubt would pass.

"I love you," he said, choosing to respond in the most honest way he knew how.

"Then that's all I need!" she exclaimed and willed herself instantly happier. "Let's do this. Take me to Gram's, I will get my things and then you can carry me over the threshold of your hotel room to our temporary home sweet home. I want this, so badly!" The change in her mood, her outlook, had convinced him to just do it. She made him happy and he wanted to do the same for her. They still had at least a few more months before Jade had to know for certain. He wanted her to be absolutely positive she could live without her baby.

***

Jade allowed herself to get swept up in how magical her first night staying with Brook was at the hotel. She was in awe of how he didn't just have a hotel room, he had a suite which was three times the size of an average hotel room and it included a kitchenette and a Jacuzzi.

Besides a slight headache, she had sobered up enough to enjoy one of the most perfect nights she had ever shared with anyone. He helped her unpack the suitcases they had retrieved from the cellar at Angie's house, and then they took a shower together. By the time they made it to the king-sized bed, their attraction overpowered how tired they both were and they ended up making love. When Jade finally fell asleep in Brock's arms, it was two-thirty in the morning.

She slept peacefully with him until his alarm sounded at five-thirty. He laid with her for a few minutes longer and then finally he got up to get ready for his work day. Brock kissed her goodbye and she fell back to sleep soon after.

A knock on the door woke her up with a start almost two hours later. Jade sat up straight in the biggest bed she had ever slept in, as the sheet fell away from her bare chest. She didn't know if she should answer the door or not, hoping it was just the maid service. The knocking persisted and then she heard her grandmother's voice. "Jadey, open this door or I will come through it!"

Jade rushed to grab a long-sleeved button down plaid shirt of Brock's that was thrown over an armchair in the corner of the room. She hurried to button it up after she pushed her arms through it. She unlocked the deadbolt on the door and opened it to find her grandmother looking far from pleased.

Angie pushed her way into the room and slammed the door behind her. "You have got to be kidding me? This? This is where you are going to hide? At least leave the fucking city as I did!" Angie's comment surprised Jade, but then again she knew her grandmother was in no position to judge her.

Jade actually giggled, but Angie was not amused. "Come in, Gram. Calm down, sit down, before you have a heart attack." Jade walked over to the window and pulled back the curtains to let the daylight shine in.

Angie did sit down, and this time she waited for Jade to speak. She was hoping for an excuse or an explanation that would mean Jade was only planning to be away for one night. Not forever.

"I know you must feel hurt, and I'm sorry I didn't tell you, Gram. I just knew you would try to talk me out of it, or hold a gun on me to force me to stay." Angie smiled at her granddaughter, the young woman who was without question her perfectly paired pea in a pod. "Does Rhett know?"

"Yes," Angie replied. "He came over, assuming he would find you and be able to drop off the baby before he went to work. I told him you had not come home and your stuff was gone. I truly felt sorry for him. He looked lost. Reminded me of Dane all those years ago when he watched me leave. You can't do this, Jadey. You just can't."

Jade wanted to ask where Aspen was right now, but she refrained. Her first step toward healing, and forgetting, was going to have to be staying out of it. If she involved herself, she would still be in the equation she had gone through emotional hell last night to subtract herself from. Her turmoil was hardly over with, she was just consciously choosing to ignore it as it attempted to slowly chip away at her.

"I need you to do something for me, Gram," Jade began. "I don't expect you to side with me on this, that wouldn't be fair. I know you understand me, though, and because you do, please just give me the support I need to get through this. Hold me if I need one of those tight, close hugs that only you can give. You know how to make me feel like my broken pieces are capable of being put back together."

"Oh Jadey," Angie's voice cracked. "You know I love you more than anything. That is why I feel so strongly about pulling you back from doing this. I did this, and I regretted it. Not right away, no, I was too self-centered and cold-hearted. You already feel torn, I can see it in your eyes. Do not ignore that, because those pangs of pain and doubt and sadness are what will keep you from walking away."

Jade was sitting close to her in side-by-side armchairs. "You had a career goal and big dreams to chase when you left, and you earned a college degree during that time. You found your passion then, and there was nothing that was going to stand in your way. I have fallen in love, and I feel passionate about never letting go of that feeling. I can't walk away from it. I won't."

"Does this man, Brock Green, not want a life with you if you keep your baby?" Angie had wondered that before now, but never asked Jade.

"He has never said that, no." Jade never asked him either. "Gram, the best day of my life happened when that man walked into it. He's my saving grace, my heart and soul, my future."

"And one day, love," Angie said, "you will realize your heart and soul is your child. There is no love, nor connection like it. Nothing compares. But, you go, chase your dream and get it out of your system. Doing that will keep you from eventually resenting that baby girl if you stay. And doing that will bring you back to her, one day." Angie wanted to add *just don't wait years*, like she had done, but how that unraveled was up to Jade. And fate.

Jade actually felt empowered by her grandmother's words which she considered to be wisdom. She was going to coast full speed ahead without guilt or regret or anything else that would make her look back.

Chapter 12

When she drove away from the hotel, Angie rolled down the driver's side window in her car. She needed some air, fresh air to slowly breathe in and out, not the air conditioning blowing from the vents. She had failed, or at least it felt as if she had. She saw this coming with Jade from the moment her baby was born. Angie would have done anything to keep her from making the same mistake as she did fifty years ago, but there was just no stopping her. Just as there was nothing and no one who could have prevented Angie from walking away back then.

She didn't cry, but she felt sad. She didn't yell, or curse the way life replicated itself sometimes, but she did feel angry. And she didn't want to hide this from her daughter. She owed it to Sher to be the one to tell her what Jade had inevitably done.

Marie Schaefer School was just two and a half miles ahead, off of Route 50. Angie parked in the lot facing the front of the school and then she walked up to the building and opened the glass door leading into the office. The first person she saw was Sher's administrative assistant. Angie momentarily flashed back in her mind to when she spent six years working as an administrative assistant for a psychiatry firm in St. Louis. She enjoyed it, she was very good at it, but eventually she realized she had bigger dreams. She wanted a career of her own. She was passionate and adamant about it then. Just like Jade now. She had bigger dreams of a different life. Angie kept that notion in the forefront of her mind as she was greeted by the woman inside the school office.

"Hello, may help you?" The woman was petite with jet black wavy hair and a friendly smile.

"I'm here to see my daughter, she's the principal," Angie responded, feeling proud. She and Sher may have been at odds for most of her life, mainly because they were such different people, but she loved that girl and she was proud to claim her.

"Oh!" the secretary replied. "I had no idea. You're Sher's mother? My goodness, you could pass for her sister."

Angie smiled, as Sher walked out of her office and into the main office. "No, look closer, she's old enough." Sher smiled and they knew instantly that she was just teasing as Angie giggled out loud. "Kim, meet my mother, Angie Roberts."

After very little small talk, Sher invited her mother into her office and closed the door behind them.

"So, this is a first. Must be serious if you're tracking me down instead of summoning me to your house." Sher wasn't worried yet, and she was trying to read any emotion whatsoever on Angie's face, but even in times of crisis Angie was very good at holding her own. Angie looked around before she sat down. The office had burgundy carpet, black leather chairs and Sher's desk was solid black. The décor was pretty much colorless, but ritzy. A lot like Sher. She was not a colorful, warm and fuzzy type of woman, but those children in that school district had her heart and she had found her niche ensuring them the best education possible.

Sher sat behind her desk when Angie sat down in a chair directly in front of it. "I wanted you to hear this from me," Angie began. "Jade left."

"What do you mean, left? I thought she and the baby were staying with you for awhile. Was it too much for you to have them there, day and night?" Sher was unnerved how Jade always turned to her grandmother and not her own mother. She, too, lived alone and her house was much bigger. She wished Jade and the baby would feel comfortable there.

"She's staying at a hotel, with her boyfriend," Angie revealed.

"And the baby?" Sher held her breath.

"The baby is with her daddy," Angie spoke softly,

hoping if she sounded calm, her daughter would remain calm.

"Oh my God!" Sher exclaimed loud enough for her secretary to hear through the closed door. So much for hoping that remaining calm would be contagious, Angie thought. "How much longer is this cowboy going to be in town? Jade is planning to leave with him, isn't she? She's serious about getting a divorce, abandoning her baby, and moving to Tennessee!" Sher still hated the word *abandon*, even after all this time.

"I'm afraid so," Angie answered, not able to make continuous eye contact with her daughter, just fleeting, as she looked down at her shoes on the floor. She was wearing white flip flops to match her white Bermuda shorts today and a black button down three-quarter-length sleeved blouse. Sher was wearing a black flowy skirt which reached her ankles, and black strappy sandals with a white sleeveless sweater. When she stood up from behind her desk, to pace the room in anger, Angie noticed how the two of them were wearing the same colors, only reversed. They were always reversed. Always on opposite sides, combating each other.

"Mom, you didn't answer me. How much longer will that fucking cowboy be in this town? How much time do we have to change Jade's mind?" Sher, so long and lean, stood directly in front of where Angie was still seated.

"At least another three months," Angie answered, "but it's no use trying to talk her out of this decision. It's something that has been weighing on her for several months. And now she has a reason to leave. She's in love." Sher rolled her eyes at her mother. "I mean it, Sher. We need to sit back and watch how this plays out."

"And what then?" Sher snapped at her mother. "We allow four years to go by?"

"That's not fair," Angie replied, still remaining calm.

"You should have been able to get through to her! Change her mind, please!" Sher knew there was nothing she could do to reach Jade, and she had counted on her mother to be able to turn this around. And, once again, her mother let her down.

"I've tried, more than you know," Angie replied. "She needs to find out for herself. I cannot tell her how to feel. I've shared my experience and my feelings with her, but it's not the same."

Sher shook her head. "Just go. Get out of my office." Angie expected as much from Sher, so she stood up and did as she asked of her. She didn't look back when she walked out and let the door slowly close behind her. At least Sher had not heard the dreadful news secondhand.

***

Jade's first night working at Shooters since she left her baby and moved into Brock Green's hotel room was beyond rough. Most of the town was talking about her and what she had done, and being in a bar where a handful of drunks who liked to gossip hung out, Jade didn't get by with smiles and polite conversation.

By the end of her shift, she was irritated with the whispers, and on the defense from the directness of others. She had been asked if she was *really going to abandon her daughter once that cowboy rides his horse back home.* One older man, after he had a few too many beers, even called her *heartless.* Jade needed the money, but she didn't know how much more harsh judgment she could take being front and center at Shooters every night.

She had called Brock to pick her up when she was ready to leave. When she saw the lights from a vehicle through the window, she went outside. She stopped walking on the sidewalk when she noticed the vehicle that pulled up was not Brock's truck. It was a Jeep. And Brock was sitting behind the wheel. The windows and the roof were open, so she spoke aloud over the engine running. "What are you doing?"

"Picking you up in your new ride," he answered, smiling as he opened the driver's side door and got out to meet her on the sidewalk.

"What?" No one had ever done anything like that for her before. When she turned sixteen, her parents suggested she spend her babysitting money to purchase an out-dated used car. She wanted a means of transportation, but she always hated that rusty, navy blue Volvo wagon with two hundred and fifty thousand miles on it. And then for the past two years she had shared another old little pickup truck with Rhett. They had talked about getting something newer, but buying formula and diapers for the baby continued to be expensive and there was just no room in their budget for a newer car.

"From me, to you, Jade. Go on, drive me around before we head back to the hotel." Brock was smiling at her as she flung her arms around his neck and squeezed him as tight as she could.

"Thank you! I don't even know what else to say. No one has ever been this good to me! I love you, Brock Green. Forever." He still had his arms wrapped around her waist as he pulled her closer to him and kissed her, after he said, "I love you, more."

Jade was sucked into her new life quickly and blissfully. She had a brand new red Jeep, access to Brock's credit cards, and plans to quit her job at Shooters. She had already given her boss one week's notice. Brock had urged her to call it quits at the bar. He had money, she didn't need to make any. He wanted to see more of her at nighttime, and he hated the way the patrons had been mistreating her ever since she left her husband and baby, especially.

Jade agreed with Brock. It was time she found a new line of work. She was done with the bar scene, but she was indecisive on what other type of career she would be successful at. She only had a high school diploma, and she told Brock as much late one night when they were sitting in the hot tub in the hotel suite.

"I'm almost twenty-six years old and if it weren't for you, I'd have no direction in my life," she told him as she sat in the water, surrounded by bubbles and wearing a new peach bikini she had purchased at Dillards in the St. Clair Square Mall today while Brock was working.

"It will all fall into place, I promise," Brock said, pulling her close and kissing her on the lips. "Look how much it has already." Jade didn't say it, but she thought how wonderful it was to not worry about money or transportation on a daily basis. She had wheels, she had money to spend, and she had a man who loved her. She hardly thought out about her old life. In fact, she should have been ashamed missing her grandmother more than her baby. "What are you thinking about?" he asked her, still sitting close to her.

"How pitiful I should feel about myself because I do not miss my old life," she admitted. "I'm thinking about a lunch date with Gram, but not at all about Aspen."

"I don't want you to think less of yourself," Brock told her. "Life happens the way it should. You were not happy. Remember that."

Chapter 13

It was like a night out which had transformed into a vacation. It had been thirteen days since Jade left her baby, and the only person in her family she had seen and talked to was her grandmother. Jade was surprised her mother had left her alone and not shown up to scream at her, or drag her back to her home on the north side of town. She also expected to hear from Rhett, and today she did.

Her cell phone was ringing in her hand when she returned to the suite after lounging in the sun by the hotel's pool. She saw it was Rhett calling, and decided to take the call from him.

Jade answered on the third ring, standing on burgundy, Berber-textured carpeted floor with cream-colored swirls. Her skin was still hot from being outside in the sun for hours so the cool, air conditioned room felt refreshing to her. She only said, *hello*, with a question in her voice as if she didn't know who was calling. What else was she supposed to say? This was a man she did marry and create a child with, although not in that order, and now she wanted no part of him in her life. Including their baby.

"Hi Jade. How are you?" Rhett had heard his wife was driving a brand new Jeep, shopping at the mall, and planning to quit tending bar at Shooters. He already assumed how she was doing while he was struggling as a single father to their baby. Rhett wished he had money, if that is what Jade needed to be happy. The money he did earn as a first-year plumber went toward paying the bills. He knew it was tough to stay afloat sometimes, but with Jade's job they were getting by. Until she left. At first he was so angry, but not anymore.

"I'm well," she replied.

So I've heard, he wanted to say. Instead, he said, "We need to talk." Jade waited for him to continue.

She wasn't going to go there again, but now she was driving on the north side of O'Fallon and back to the home she had shared with Rhett and their baby. The hot summer air was blowing through her hair, covering her shoulders, in the open Jeep as she pulled into the rock driveway. She had been gone just a day short of two weeks, and while she never thought she would return she reminded herself that Rhett promised her *closure* as she shut the driver's side door and walked toward the house. She wouldn't just walk in, but how weird would it be to knock on that front door, she thought, as she felt confident in a new short, yellow sundress with dark brown ankle wrap sandals. Her hair looked blonder from all of her time spent in the sun at the hotel's swimming pool. Jade knew she looked good and she felt fabulous. She just hoped seeing Rhett again would not bring her back to the slump she was in. She hated her life there and as she stepped up onto the small front porch, Rhett opened the door.

First, he only stared. He almost couldn't believe the change in her, although he had gradually seen it happening once she began cheating on him with another man. "Hi, come in," he finally said, as she obliged.

Jade immediately glanced around. The baby swing in the living room was empty. The beige carpeted floor looked as if it had been freshly vacuumed, and there were no baby toys, or baby, in sight. Jade breathed a sigh of relief, and hoped Aspen was napping. She should have felt guilty, but she didn't. She just didn't want to stir any emotions she had succeeded at suppressing since the day she left.

"She's not here. My mom has her," Rhett read her mind. He had taken the morning off of work to take care of this business with Jade. When he called her yesterday, he made it hard for her to refuse to see him. The word closure seemed to appeal to her.

Jade remained standing in the living room, near the front door. She noticed Rhett was in his usual work uniform. "Have a seat," Rhett said, as he walked into the living room and picked up a few papers from on top of the coffee table. Jade sat down, gracefully in her short sundress, and waited for him to speak.

"I hired a lawyer," Rhett began. "Since we have not been married for an entire year yet, we can sever our marriage fairly quickly with an annulment." Jade was surprised by Rhett's cooperation. She also felt somewhat relieved. She wanted to be free of her old life so she could begin a new one with Brock. She only nodded her head as Rhett continued. "I also have some papers for you to sign to give up your rights to Aspen."

"What?" Jade interrupted, and surprised herself with her reaction. *Had she not already given up her rights? Isn't that exactly what she wanted?*

Rhett remained standing with the papers still in his hands. "You had an affair while we were married and then you abandoned our baby. You wanted out, you got out, and now I'm giving you a free pass to stay away forever. Or rather, I'm ensuring that you can never come back and fuck up my life ever again. I intend, someday, to move on. Remarry, maybe. Have more children, hopefully. I don't want to ever be worried about having to look over my shoulder, wondering if you will come back into town with the intent of playing mother again. You are, afterall, so much like your Gramma."

Jade could not believe his words. It was obvious he had been coached by someone, probably his parents, she thought. And then she questioned why she was allowing him, and this offer of his, to get to her. Signing those papers should not bother her if she really wanted to move on with her life and never look back.

"I will need to read over the papers, for a day or so," she responded.

"Okay, I guess," he said. "Take your time, but don't take too much. I hear your boyfriend only has a couple of months left in this town." Rhett was callous, but he had a right to be, Jade thought. She did *fuck up* his life. She did the same to her own, too, and that's why she wanted out. She was about to leave all of that in the past, with Rhett's help. All she had to do was sign the papers.

***

It shouldn't have bothered her so much. She found herself thinking too hard, dwelling, as she sped through the side streets and back onto Route 50. When she reached her hotel, she sat down by the table near the kitchenette inside of her room. She pulled the papers out of her designer handbag, another new item she had just purchased. And then she began to read.

Custodial parent, Rhett P. Connors is seeking termination of parental rights for Aspen Angela Connors who no longer has a relationship with non-custodial parent, Jade A. Connors. If the non-custodial parent agrees to terminate her parental rights, child support obligations will cease.

The court will focus on the best interest of the child to consider termination of parental rights. However, courts prefer not to terminate parental rights. It is considered a last resort. Unless a child is in a dangerous situation, or someone is willing to adopt a child, a court would prefer to avoid terminating a biological parent's rights. Instead, courts will attempt to accommodate a parent's needs and wishes, to the furthest extent necessary. In this case, Jade A. Connors is at fault of abandonment of Aspen Angela Connors. The child's father, Rhett P. Connors is vying for sole parental rights.

Jade stopped reading and pushed the papers away from her on the table top. This felt different to her now. It was her choice to leave. It was something she wanted to do for a very long time. And, now, she was being forced to make it official. It no longer felt on her terms, and it also felt terribly final. *What if Dane had done the same to Angie all those years ago? What would have happened to her mother and her aunt?* Jade's thoughts were racing. Rhett definitely had the final word with this document, and now she was at a loss for what to do.

Any time in her life when she was troubled, she turned to the one person who could always help her figure it out. Jade was back behind the wheel of her Jeep and on Smiley Street again. It was a road she could travel blindfolded. Rain or shine, snow or ice, Jade had made it to her grandmother's house over the years in all conditions. Today, she traveled that road with a heavy heart because she knew, before long, she would be too far away to make it to Angie's house in only a matter of minutes.

Jade found her working in the flower garden in the backyard. She was wearing a purple tank top with wide straps and faded cut-off jean shorts with purple flip flops to match on her feet. Jade smiled at her before Angie knew she was there. That was her Gram. Ageless. Beautiful. And rocking a golden summer tan from her gardening hobby.

106

Before Jade interrupted her, Angie looked up and saw her. "Oh Jadey, it's good to see you." Angie's smile lit up her eyes, but behind her happiness, she was worried about this girl.

"Good to see you, too, Gram," Jade responded, still looking chic, dressed in her yellow sundress.

"You're taking good care of yourself," Angie said, noticing her new clothes, bronzed skin, highlighted hair, and hot pink polished nails and toes. It felt good for Angie to see Jade looking well. Better than well. For so long, she was depressed and couldn't have cared less if she had gotten dressed or even brushed her hair.

"I am, Gram. I'm happy," Jade said, walking over to the swing in the yard where they sat down in unison, beside each other.

"That's good to hear," Angie said, patting her on the bare leg after she had taken off her green gardening gloves and placed them on the swing beside her. Given the situation, Angie didn't ask any questions yet. She waited for Jade to tell her what was weighing on her mind.

"I'm going to miss you when I move to Tennessee with Brock," Jade said, feeling teary-eyed.

"I'll miss you more," Angie responded, taking ahold of Jade's hand, "but it will be okay, the distance between us I mean, if I know you are happy. Truly happy."

"I think I will be, I am now, and it can only get better, right?" Jade smiled and Angie nodded her head.

"Right, if you can live without your baby," she said, honestly.

"Did you think about yours while you were gone for all those years?" Jade asked her.

"I did. I don't think I'd be human if I had not. I wondered about them, yes. I just never wanted to go back. I felt like they deserved better, and quite honestly I believed it was up to me to make myself happy. And, at the time, I was not happy being a mother to those two babies." Angie didn't know any other way to speak to Jade about this subject. She had to speak from her heart.

"Thank you for putting it into words for me, Gram. I'm not an awful person. You never were either. We're just different." Angie giggled a little and Jade joined her.

"Just take this one day at a time, and don't tell your mother I said that," Angie stated.

"I haven't seen mom. Does she know? She has to know by now, the whole town knows." Jade was no longer embarrassed or ashamed. She only felt that way when she was working at Shooters and around the gossip, the stares, and the judging. Her job there was now done.

"I told her, and I have not seen or heard from her since," Angie answered. "It's typical of Sher. She needs time."

"I want to say goodbye to her before I leave," Jade said.

"Of course, and you should." A part of Angie still wanted to fight this, shake some sense into Jade. She swore she would not let this happen, but now she felt like there was nothing she could say or do to change Jade's mind so she just wanted to be there for her.

"I saw Rhett this morning. He called me and asked me to come to the house." Angie's eyes widened as Jade spoke. She wondered if Jade saw the baby. "I went there because he didn't sound angry on the phone, and he said we needed closure and he had found a way to give us that. Our marriage of ten and a half months can be annulled quickly, and I have those papers to sign. He also gave me papers to give up my rights as Aspen's mother."

"What? No!" Angie reacted immediately. "Please tell me that you did not sign them!"

"I didn't. Not yet. I told him I needed to read them over."

"It's too final that way, Jadey," Angie told her. "You will change your mind one day, I know you will. Tear up those papers. End your marriage, but don't sign off your rights to Aspen. Maybe you will, maybe you won't, but, one day, you could have a change of heart."

"A change of heart," Jade repeated Angie's words. "You are amazing, do you know that? You always know the right thing to say, exactly what I need."

"I think that's because we are one in the same, Jadey," Angie smiled at her granddaughter as Jade put her arm around her shoulders.

"It's going to be okay, Gram. Better than okay. I know it will."

***

That evening, Jade shared the legal papers with Brock. They had just eaten dinner at the table in their hotel suite as they decided to stay in and order take-out meals from Bella Milano, a local Italian restaurant.

"So the annulment looks like it will be quick and painless," he said, and then he flipped through the other set of papers lying beside their Styrofoam containers on the tabletop. "Rhett seems to want you out now. He's not fighting to keep you in his life, or his daughter's. How do you feel about that?"

"I don't think it's fair for me to have to sign those papers," she said quietly, wondering if he was going to call her out on being indecisive.

Brock nodded his head. "Well if you feel that way, it's a good thing you didn't sign the papers on the spot. Think on it."

"I don't have to think about ending my marriage. That was over a long time ago. I want a future with you." Jade looked directly at him, and he smiled.

"Me too, and we are going to have a happy life together. This weekend will be just the start of all the good things to come," Brock told her.

"What's this weekend?" Jade asked him, feeling excited.

"I'm taking you home with me, back to Franklin, Tennessee."

"Are you serious?" Jade asked him, jumping out of her chair and onto his lap and he wrapped his arms around her.

"Pack your bags, darlin', we're going on a road trip." Brock kissed her long and hard and Jade, once again, found herself feeling completely swept away. Being with this man was like being right smack in the middle of a fairytale.

***

The Saturday morning drive to Brock's home in the south took five hours. They talked, laughed, and listened to country music on satellite radio the whole way there. Jade was accustomed to country music and its established artists. In Shooters, many of the regular patrons played their same favorite artists on the old jukebox in the corner of the bar. Clint Black. Lorrie Morgan. Randy Travis. Tanya Tucker. Alan Jackson. George Jones. Tammy Wynette. They all sang of heartbreak, big dreams, and fallen stars. Jade was caught up in the magic of how every good country song told a story. Her life had not been easy, but she couldn't help but feel like everything was about to turn around for her. Starting with love. She was madly in love with Brock Green and could not wait to learn more about him. His home. His family. Who and what made him the man he had become.

The moment they drove twenty miles south of downtown Nashville, Tennessee into a charming subdivision nestled inside of the City of Franklin, Jade was in awe. The homes looked historic, but they were brand new with a level of quality, sophistication and authenticity in their architecture. Those homes were preserving the past and ensuring the future with their classic design elements. In middle Tennessee, Brock lived in a home that had a classic, symmetrical design, with high windows, tall white columns and an exquisitely detailed outside frame. It stood two stories tall with white siding, and an upper balcony above the front porch which was wrapped entirely around the front and sides of the house. Four white, high-back wooden rocking chairs were placed to the left and right of the front door, two on each side. The shutters were painted tungsten metallic, black or brown depending on how the sun shone on it, and the landscape around the house was breathtaking with greens and flowers of every color accenting the trees and the bushes.

The pavement leading up to the house formed a circle and Brock parked directly in front. There was a detached triple-car garage nearby which looked as big as a house. It was easily bigger than the house Jade had been living in.

"You're awfully quiet," Brock said, looking over at her as she stared out the truck window.

"I'm overwhelmed with all the beauty," Jade said, quietly and completely taken by what she was seeing.

"Welcome to the South," Brock said, grinning, as he opened his truck door. "Let me show you around."

First, he walked her around on the grounds. There were trails, expansive fields, an eleven-acre lake where Brock said he liked to fish and Jade saw his canoe docked. She admired the gazebo near the lake but her desired sight was the resort-style swimming pool she saw behind the house as they walked back.

"Is this for real? Are you for real? This is all yours, Brock Green?" Jade was in awe, to say the least. Being there, knowing she was going to live there, was a dream.

"It's real, and believe me when I say that I will do everything I can to make you happy here." Brock had stopped walking and he was facing her. He was wearing his jeans, boots, and a tight red crewneck t-shirt. He didn't have a hat on his head and Jade loved how his hair was growing out and wavy around his ears and bangs.

"I am happy when I'm with you," she told him. "I was happy laying beside you on that old leather couch in the backroom of a bar. I'm happy shacking up in a hotel with you," she smiled. "Don't you see? It's you and you alone. All of this," she held out her arms and twirled around, "is not something I have to have."

"Okay then I'll sell and move your ass to a one-room shack on the outskirts of town," he teased her, and she responded, "Don't you dare!" Truth be told, Jade was taken by both Brock and everything he owned.

The interior of the house was even more breathtaking for Jade to see, one room at a time. There were dark polished wooden floorboards which contrasted beautifully with the white walls, cabinets and ceilings. She counted four bedrooms, just as many baths, all with high ceilings and stunning polished floors. The master bedroom and bathroom were both white and decorated combined with a classic chic style and modern flair. Jade could not believe all of it. Every room she entered had plenty of windows which allowed for a view of the greenery outside.

"So, you like?" Brock asked her as he pulled her down onto the king-sized bed with a canopy, and white everything. Jade's eyes were wide looking at it all.

"How do you pay for all of this? I want to be a construction foreman," she teased, and Brock laughed out loud as he propped himself up on one elbow while laying beside her.

"The company is family-owned. My father and my mother own it, I just help run it," Brock explained. "We build homes like this all over Tennessee and we do special projects all over the country." Brock went on to explain how his father was

summoned by an old friend of his to take part in the
construction of a multi-million dollar Department of Defense
building on Scott Air Force Base. He told Jade how his father
was past the point in his career of wanting to handle the stress
of an on-location project, five hours away from home, so Brock
agreed to spearhead it.

"How come you didn't tell me all of this before?" Jade
asked him.

"Because some women see dollar signs. I've learned to
find out who a woman is, what's really inside her heart, before I
take her home." Brock smiled at Jade and he moved close
enough to pull her into a kiss, but he stopped when she spoke.

"I don't have much to show for," Jade said, sincerely.
"Don't get me wrong, I could get used to this life, real quick, but
it's not something I have to have." And Brock knew that. He had
realized as much about Jade from the moment he met her. He
wanted to be with her and he wanted to share his life, a life of
luxury, with her.

He began to unbutton the powder blue sleeveless blouse
she was wearing with a short, ruffled white skirt. Her full
breasts were spilling out of the top of her white-laced bra. She
slipped off her white ankle-wrap sandals and they landed on
the floor beside the bed. He touched her breasts through the
lace and kissed her hard and full on the mouth as she reached
for the button fly on his jeans. And what followed was
passionate, explosive love-making under the canopy in Brock
Green's bed.

Chapter 14

Three-hundred miles northwest, back home, Sher was beside herself with a crying baby. She had tried everything to calm Aspen, and now she was driving down Smiley Street toward her mother's house.

Angie could hear the baby screaming from inside of her house so she swiftly opened the door as Sher came barging in with the baby, upright in her arms. Aspen's face was red and wet with tears. And Sher didn't look much better. She wore a look of panic on her own flushed face.

"What is going on?" Angie asked over the noise of shrieking cries.

"I don't know! I offered to watch her whenever Rhett needed help. He asked me to keep her tonight, overnight, and she has been screaming at me since her daddy left!" First, Angie was proud of Sher for wanting to be present in Aspen's life. Finally. That baby girl needed the presence of a woman now more than ever.

Angie hurried over to her sofa and took a blanket off of the back of it. She spread it out onto her open living room floor and walked over to a white wicker basket she had sitting near her magazine rack alongside of her recliner chair. In it, she had some toys and books that Jade had left behind when she and Aspen were temporarily living there.

Sher followed her mother's lead and set the baby down on the blanket. Less than a minute later, Aspen's crying ceased and the toys which were familiar to her were now in her hands.

"How did you just do that?" Sher asked, backing away from the blanket and the baby.

"It's this house, the toys, me. She's familiar," Angie told her daughter, an adult who still seemed like a defiant child to her in so many ways. "She needs to get to know you. I want you to stay here for awhile tonight. I want to help you with her, but then you need to take her home with you so you can make memories with her there. It's not too late to be her grandma," Angie said to Sher, and she listened without rolling her eyes or making a snide remark.

An hour later, the baby was asleep on the blanket on the floor, amidst the toys, as Sher sat on the end of the sofa and Angie in her recliner. "She seems happy," Sher said, referring to the baby. "I mean, before the screaming, when Rhett brought her over, and again now as she was playing and interacting with you. I wonder if she misses Jade?"

This was a dodgy subject for Sher to bring up. Treading anywhere near the issue of abandonment always ended up with her throwing stones in the form of hurtful words she could never take back.

"Rhett is a good father to her," Angie began. "He always has been. We have all witnessed how Jade was with her baby, too. I can't see where Aspen would miss her when she never allowed her to see her true, loving self. Something kept her from adoring and mothering that child. It was out of her control." Angie wanted to say she understood that feeling, but she refrained.

"Jade is her mother, and regardless of how many kisses she never gave her, Aspen knows she's gone. I know because since as far back as I can recall, I missed you." This was just as painful for Sher to say as it was for Angie to hear.

"Let's just hope and pray, if you do that sort of thing, that Jade comes to her senses one day. I know I was four years too late, but I think even with a late start I managed to make up for most of our lost time. I just think you, especially, at times felt confused by your father's grief and your so-called hatred for me. The line between the two blurred and I'm not sure it's all that clear still today."

Sher shook her head. "Jesus, mother. You really were born to be a shrink. Too bad that didn't quite pan out."

Angie winked at her. "If it had panned out, I would have been even later getting back to where I belonged."

"You at least finally were able to admit you belonged with your children," Sher said. "I wish you could bottle that potion and force Jade to drink it."

"You and I both know there's no forcing Jade to do anything," Angie stated, and Sher nodded her head before she replied, "I wonder who she inherited that from," with a crooked smile.

***

Jade woke up to the sun coming through the open white wide-slab wooden blinds in the window. She reached for Brock, but only felt her hand on the sheets. Her eyes were closed, but they popped open when she wondered why he had gotten up without waking her.

As she sat upright in bed, the white sheet fell from her bare chest. She remembered their love making in that canopy bed yesterday, and again last night. He was a man who was attentive to her needs in the bedroom and as her mind went there, she was missing him.

Before she moved from the bed, Brock came walking in the room, wearing only a pair of blue and white checkered boxers, and carrying a tray with a rose in a vase and two plates of food. "Good morning, love of my life," he said, sitting down on the bed beside her.

"Breakfast in bed?" she asked, looking at the toasted English muffins piled with scrambled eggs and melted cheese on top of those. "No one has ever done this for me before."

"Well consider it the first of many firsts," Brock said, smiling at her as he helped himself to the breakfast he wanted to share with her. She started eating, too, and again she felt happier than she ever had.

After they ate breakfast in bed, Brock told her he had to meet his father at the office for awhile, and he suggested she enjoy the pool or take one of his cars in the garage out shopping.

"One of the cars?" she asked him, thinking of her Jeep back home, too.

"Yes, dear. I have more." Brock smiled at her and he kissed her on the cheek before he started to get up out of bed.

"Whoa, that's it? A kiss on the cheek?" Jade stopped him from moving any further away from her. "That's all I get to hold me over for hours?" Brock laughed out loud before he came back to bed, and said, "Oh you poor little thing," as he pulled back the sheet, away from her naked body, and she reached down to take off his boxers.

***

After she showered, Jade slipped on one of the bikinis she packed for the weekend. Her size six body was in the best shape it's ever been. She had only gained twenty pounds during her pregnancy and lost the weight within weeks after Aspen was born. Since she met Brock, she had been paying more attention to taking exceptional care of herself. She now felt shapely and toned and she looked it, too. Her bikini was all black and she wore a white sheer cover up over top before going downstairs and outside to the pool. She took a towel out of the linen closet in the bathroom to bring with her to the pool. As she left the bedroom that they would soon call *theirs*, Jade noticed the closed doors in the hallway again. Yesterday, when Brock gave her the grand tour through all of the rooms, she remembered four. But, there were five. Not that it mattered how many there were, but there was a room on the end which she knew she had not gone into. The door was closed, just like all of the others, and maybe they had gone inside of that room too. She could have lost count, which would be understandable in a house so immense. Jade didn't think twice, she just went to the door, turned the knob and peeked her head inside. The room was completely empty. She walked all the way in and stood in the center of a room with yet another high ceiling, white walls, and dark hardwood flooring. It was strange seeing nothing in it when all of the other rooms were completely furnished. For a moment, Jade stood barefoot in her bikini and cover up in the middle of the room, and when she started to walk out she turned her head and noticed a door. She assumed it was for a closet and when her curiosity peaked, she turned the knob. And then she discovered it was locked.

Jade allowed her imagination to wander for a moment. Everyone harbored pain, or even secrets, but Brock was an honest man. The most honest she had ever met. It was none of her business what was stored in that closet, and she wouldn't waste anymore time dwelling on it. She left the room and shut the door again. She had her towel for the swimming pool draped over her forearm and her sunglasses were resting on top of her head, nestled in between the knot of blonde hair piled up on top.

When she reached the top of the stairs, she was taken aback when she saw a woman coming up toward her. She was wearing a short, white eye-lit shift dress and thick, block-heeled red sandals. Her hair was as blonde as Jade's, she noticed, as the two women met at the top of the stairs.

"Hello," Jade said, looking as confused as she felt. She assumed Brock had staff in that house at times to keep it all as immaculate as it looked. He had been gone for months and everything inside of the house including the grounds and the pool outside all obviously were well kept, daily. But, this woman hardly looked like she was hired help.

"Well, hi there," the woman replied as if she was accustomed to running into just anyone in that house.

"I'm Jade..." Jade said, not knowing what else to say or whether or not she should add, *Brock's girlfriend.* Just the thought of that, knowing she was *his,* made her feel alive and happy inside.

"Of course you are!" the woman responded with what Jade thought was a little too much enthusiasm. "My son has told me so much about you."

Son? Jade felt her face flush. She couldn't see a resemblance, but she could see a beautiful, well-maintained woman who looked to be, maybe, in her early fifties. Brock was thirty-one years old so Jade could see this woman being his mother, but the idea of his mother standing before her right now made her incredibly nervous. *What exactly had he told his mother about her? That she was a bartender? Left her husband? Abandoned her baby? Damn, a woman like her must think her son had found a real prize.* Jade pushed those thoughts out of her mind and continued to appear confident on the exterior. She was young, beautiful, and wearing an expensive swimsuit, *thank God with a cover up on at this moment,* her nails and hair were done, and her skin was as bronzed as this woman's.

"Mrs. Green? Oh my, it's a pleasure to meet you. You have raised an amazing son." Jade didn't want to overdo it, say too much, appear to be brownnosing. But, she did mean her every word.

Mrs. Green offered her hand first, and Jade carefully, gently, received it with a sincere smile. She had poker straight hair, cut at an angle just under her cheek bone. Those cheek bones were prominent on her flawless face. It was like looking at Barbie, two or three decades later.

"Please, call me Karla." Karla knew Jade would be at the house. She was overjoyed to have seen and spoken to her son at the office when he showed up there this morning. Karla was always at their office. She was the president and co-owner, with her husband, of Green Construction. It was her daddy's money which enabled Clay Green to launch his own construction company that had thrived beyond expectation. The company would one day be Brock's. He had worked tirelessly under the vice president's title, and since he was their only child, it would all be his. Karla Green wanted, more than anything, for her son to marry and start a family, to give her and Clay grandchildren and eventually heirs to the company they had put blood, sweat, and tears, into.

Karla tried too hard with the last woman in Brock's life. She knew that, she recognized how she had pushed. Now, she wanted to welcome Jade but not overwhelm her. She had seen something different in her son's eyes this time. Sometimes a person just knows when they've met *the one*, and it clearly shows. That's an answered prayer for any mother for her son. "I don't mean to invade your privacy," Karla said, still standing with Jade at the top of the stairs. "I'm just here to retrieve something from the office." Jade remembered seeing the office upstairs in one of the rooms when Brock had given her the grand tour.

"You're fine. I'm a guest here in this beautiful house. Brock said he would be back in a few hours so I was just going to wait for him by the pool." Jade pulled the two sides of her cover-up together, despite the fact that it was sheer and Karla Green could see right through it.

"Of course, feel free, and no need to cover up that body. You're beautiful. Just wait until you get to be my age, it takes work and a lot of money for upkeep." Karla smiled at her, her teeth were perfectly straight and bright white.

Jade let out a giggle before she added, "You look like you could be Brock's sister, not his mother."

And that was a winning compliment. It certainly won over Karla Green. She liked this girl.

Chapter 15

The sun on her skin felt heavenly as she laid back in a lounge chair with her eyes closed behind her large, dark sunglasses. The bubbling sound of the water jets pumping in the pool relaxed her. Jade was thinking of nothing and no one. She was relishing the luxury she had right at this moment.

She had not gotten into the pool yet, she planned to step in when she reached the point of needing to cool down. She thought about going inside to get something to eat or drink soon. Her stomach and lower abdomen felt crampy, and most likely she needed to refuel her body as she had not eaten since breakfast.

Several minutes passed before Jade felt a trickle on her inner thigh. Because she had not gotten wet, her skin and swimsuit were dry. It could have been sweat, but Jade opened her eyes to be sure and that's when she saw red. Blood was trickling down her leg and Jade felt panicked, immediately. She jumped to her feet, grabbing her towel. She was relieved that she had not gotten any on the expensive patio furniture as she dabbed her leg with the towel in her hands. It was not time for her period. She just had one two weeks ago, she thought. She was accustomed to spotting during ovulation sometimes, but this seemed to be a little much and it alarmed her. She went inside and upstairs to the master bathroom. She took a shower to feel clean and then retrieved a tampon from her handbag. The timing of the spotting annoyed her. Brock would be home soon and the last thing she wanted was a third party. They still were at the stage in their relationship where intimacy happened often. Known to have sporadic spotting, Jade put it out of her mind and got dressed. Wearing cut-off denim shorts and a white v-neck t-shirt, she was just about to leave the bedroom to go downstairs to the kitchen for something to eat when Brock walked in.

"Well, hello there, beautiful. You're dressed perfectly for the afternoon adventure that I have planned," Brock smiled at her and kissed her gently on the lips. She responded and then reached for the large shopping bag he had in his hand. She didn't recognize the name of the store on the bag, so she immediately looked inside as Brock laughed at her eagerness for his surprise.

"For me?" Jade asked, as she pulled out a pair of light brown cowboy boots with purple rhinestone trim and slipped them on with her shorts. She felt cute and she looked it, too.

"For you," he answered. "We're going riding."

Jade was both nervous and excited anticipating her first time on a horse as she and Brock walked the grounds toward the twelve-stall barn. Brock took her by the hand as they walked.

"I'm riding on the back of yours, right?" Jade asked him.

"What if I give you the tamest horse I have?" he asked her.

"Not for my first time!" Jade reacted. Getting to know Brock's lifestyle amazed her, but she couldn't have cared less about learning to ride a horse.

"You hate horses?" he asked, teasing her as he pretended to have his feelings hurt.

"I can't say for sure," she said. "It's not something I've ever been introduced to. I'll give it a chance as long as you're with me."

Brock smiled at her and put his arm around her. "Baby, I love you, but I don't trust you with my horses. Not yet."

She never tired of hearing him tell her he loved her. "I love you, too," she giggled and teased, "but not your horses."

They were almost to the stables when Brock spoke again. "So, you met my mama today, huh?"

Jade smiled first. She was impressed with that woman, and a little flattered because they had been talking about her at the office. She just hoped Brock had not told his mother all about her failed marriage and choice to walk away from her baby. "She's beautiful and she was very kind to me."

Brock smiled, "Good, I'm hoping the two of you continue the mutual admiration as we all have dinner plans tonight."

***

Clay Green stood as tall as his son, just under six-foot. He was fuller in his face, through his shoulders, and his belly. Brock was his father's son in appearance. Their hair was the same, grown out on the sides and bangs, only Clay's was graying a little in his mid-fifties. Neither one of them were wearing their cowboy hats tonight as they dined with both Jade and Karla. Jade was wearing a strapless white sundress with a pair of chunky-heeled white sandals. Her tan from being poolside today made her look even more stunning. Her hair was down, curled and on her shoulders tonight. Karla looked equally as radiant in a little sleeveless black dress and strappy gold sandals.

The four of them were seated at a quiet table at the Red Pony, one of the finest restaurants in Franklin. The conversation was easy, as Jade listened and spoke in turn. His mother was a woman who liked to talk. Karla Green was extremely proud of her son, her only child. She also liked to talk about herself. Jade was interested and fully engulfed in being with all of them. Until the focus turned to her. She didn't have anything to brag about, and she was still unsure of how much Brock had already told his parents about her.

Jade had told them she, too, was an only child, her parents were divorced, her mother was a school principal and her aunt was a psychiatrist. She also spoke highly of her grandmother, and mentioned how she was the most important person in the world to her.

When Karla asked Jade what she does for a living, Brock interrupted. "She managed a restaurant, similar to this caliber. She recently resigned when I invited her to stay at my hotel with me and return here, to Franklin, to live. Call me selfish, but managing a restaurant at nighttime took her away from me." Karla giggled at her son's comment and his father appeared proud of how his son wanted to take care of his woman.

"Well, the reason I ask is we, Clay and I, would like to present an offer to you, Jade," Karla spoke with a business tone. "When you move here, a position will be yours at Green Construction, if you accept. With your management experience and people skills, we think you will excel working for us."

Jade didn't know what to say. She was a bartender. Yes, she managed the bar, solo each and every night, but it was hardly upscale and now she felt like she should be embarrassed because obviously Brock was. "I will consider your offer, thank you," Jade replied, making fleeting eye contact between Karla, Clay, and the glass of wine she now took in her hand and began to take a long drink from. She wanted to hide behind that glass, or better yet crawl under the table.

Their evening ended with Brock's parents after dinner. They had driven separately and met at the restaurant so when Brock and Jade got into his truck to drive home, she sat in silence and he immediately noticed. "You okay?" he asked her as they began to drive back to Brock's home.

"Just overwhelmed," Jade answered.

"By getting to know my parents?" Brock asked her.

"By your parents, especially your mother, wanting to get to know me." Jade was being honest. If she could not be herself with those people, how could she ever truly fit in?

"If you're upset about what I told her, the little white lie, believe me it was necessary. My mother can be something else sometimes. She has money and class and I just don't want her to not give you a chance because of the fact that we met in a bar when you served me a beer."

"It's who I am, or who I was," Jade looked down at the floor board where she had slipped her bare feet out of her chunky-heeled white sandals.

"Hey," Brock said, rubbing her bare knee with his right hand as he drove with his left. "I love everything about you, please know that. It's my mother who can be judgy, that's all." When Jade didn't reply, Brock slowed his truck and pulled off the road to park on the shoulder. "Talk to me," he said putting his arm around her upper back.

"Your mother doesn't know, does she?" Jade asked.

"No," Brock replied. "It's none of her business that you were unhappy in your marriage, or how your heart was not into being a mother. That does not define who you are, Jade. I mean that."

"Thank you," she replied, feeling extremely grateful for this man in her life. He understood her. "I just felt like you were embarrassed by me."

"Not at all," he said. "I just see your situation as private. I mean, you are still trying to figure out what you want." Jade assumed he meant whether or not to sign those papers to terminate her parental rights to her child.

"Do you think I should sign the papers?" Jade asked him. She had not been thinking about that at all during this trip, but now it was back in the forefront of her mind. There was no

LORI BELL

room for Aspen in the life she wanted with Brock. She knew that now. A part of her didn't want to return to O'Fallon. Ever. She wanted to erase the past and seize the present. Her new life awaited in Tennessee with Brock. But, Jade knew Brock had to return to the jobsite on Scott Air Force Base for another couple of months and she had to find closure. Maybe Rhett's offer was exactly what she needed to finally move on.

"I think that is your decision and yours alone. I will support you, whatever you decide," Brock told her as they remained parked on the road's shoulder and cars passed by.

"Brock, be honest with me about something."

"Always," he said.

"Do you want children of your own someday?" It was the question she knew would come up eventually and now seemed like a suitable time to ask.

"I have something I want to share with you," he said, shifting his truck into drive and pulling back onto the road.

When they arrived back at his house, Brock led the way upstairs and Jade followed him. They were standing in the middle of that empty room Jade had found and been in this morning. Then, he began to tell Jade a story about the woman in his life, just before her.

There was hurt in his eyes when he explained how this woman, Pamela he called her, was pregnant. He cared about her, he said, but he didn't love her. But, her being pregnant had changed everything. He wanted to do right by her, by his child, and marry her.

Jade listened raptly as Brock continued to explain. "We never got married," he said.

130

"And the baby?" Jade interrupted.

"Wasn't mine," Brock added.

"Oh my God," Jade said, reaching for both of Brock's hands with her own as they stood in the middle of the empty room with dark hardwood floors, white walls and white doors.

"She wanted it all, she wanted this life," Brock stated. "She tried to pass off another man's child as mine."

"So what happened?" Jade asked him.

"I kicked her out," he replied, walking over to the closed closet door as he reached above its doorframe and retrieved a key. Jade's eyes widened as she thought of turning the doorknob to that closet door this morning. "And I kept everything that was in this room and ready for the baby to be born." Brock unlocked and opened the door and Jade followed him into the walk-in closet which was half the size of the room they had just been standing in. First, Jade saw a mattress, small enough for a crib, leaning up against the wall. Then, with it, she saw a headboard, footboard, and the rails for the sides of a crib. There was a chest of drawers in there too, and when Jade looked inside she saw full drawers of baby clothes, bibs, burp rags, and onesies, mostly all blue.

"I thought I was going to have a son," Brock spoke with that same look of pain in his eyes. "I was excited about becoming a father."

"But you didn't love her," Jade said, knowing exactly what that felt like with Rhett.

"No, I didn't, which is exactly my point of bringing you in here tonight. You asked me if I wanted children and I have an answer for you. First and foremost, I want a woman who makes me feel how you make me feel. I want to love her like there is no tomorrow and not worry about those tomorrows that lie ahead. What is important to me is sharing my life with you, and whatever happens, happens."

Jade was teary-eyed as she looked at him and listened to his heartfelt words. "So why have you kept all of this stuff?"

"Maybe as a reminder not to let just any woman into my life again. Maybe as a way of hoping one day I will have a use for all of those little things locked in there. I don't know, Jade, I really don't."

"Why did you let me into your heart so easily?" Jade asked him.

"Because when I saw you, I knew," he answered. "I knew it did not matter to you where I come from, or what I own." Jade smiled at him and he moved toward her and kissed her hard on the mouth. "I love you," he said with a wanting look in his eyes.

"I love you, too," she responded as they backed out of the closet and ended up in each other's arms on the floor, in the middle of that empty room. He unzipped the back of her strapless sundress and she quickly took off his starched white shirt, popping off the last two buttons. She thought of the tampon she had removed in the bathroom of the restaurant when she pleasantly discovered she was no longer spotting. She hoped that was still the case as Brock's hands and lips were on her body and a very short time later he plunged inside of her and rocked over her on his knees as she laid on the wood flooring with her legs up and bent. He momentarily pulled out and she glanced for blood. There was none. She then turned around and positioned herself on her hands and knees as he swiftly took her from behind. He plunged hard and deeper with each motion as Jade climaxed with him still inside of her, moaning his name loudly as he came after her and then laid down next to her, wrapping her up in his arms.

***

In the middle of a sound sleep, Jade abruptly sat upright in Brock's bed. He had been asleep beside her, but he woke up when she yelled out "Oh my God, help!" just before she fell back onto her pillow and lost consciousness. In her sleep, she had felt the blood pooling underneath her and onto her upper legs. From what she could see in the dark room, she was lying in blood from the waist down. The abdominal pain, and that sight, caused her to black out. Brock jumped up out of the bed and turned on the ceiling fan's light directly above them. He saw the blood. It was on him too. He called her name, but she did not move. Her face was as white as the pillowcase her head was lying on. Brock panicked and went to her, but she was unresponsive. He grabbed his cell phone off of the nightstand beside the bed and called 911.

The dispatcher assured him an ambulance was on its way, and they wanted him to remain on the line, but he dropped the phone onto the floor as he rushed into the bathroom to get run cold water over a wash cloth and then hurried back to the bed to make the woman he loved come back to him.

Jade was drifting in and out of consciousness and Brock didn't know what to do. He was covered in blood now and so was she. Some of it was from him touching her face and her hands and trying to reach her, help her, keep her from dying on him. It was the scariest thing he had ever experienced and when the paramedics arrived, they pushed him aside to attempt to stabilize Jade before rushing her off to the hospital.

Chapter 16

Brock had managed to pull on a pair of jeans, a cobalt blue t-shirt and his boots barefoot, just minutes before traveling directly behind the ambulance in his truck. The paramedics would not allow him to ride with them as they had continued to work on Jade. She had lost a lot of blood. And, the expressions on their faces, as they hauled her away on top of that stretcher, sent sheer panic through Brock's body.

"Save her!" he yelled aloud and alone in his dark truck as he drove equally as fast as the ambulance. He pounded his hands on the steering wheel and his voice cracked. "God, you have to save her!"

***

Brock's face was in his hands as he sat bent forward in a chair in the waiting room. The blood had dried on his hands and he could smell it. He felt helpless. It had been too long. He had not heard anything from anyone. He was trying to keep calm, but all he wanted to do was lose his temper and demand to see the woman he loved.

He looked up from his hands as the doctor walked through the open doorway. "Mr. Green?" He knew that was him. All the staff had been referring to him as *the man covered in dried blood.*

Brock looked up quickly and then stood up. The doctor, who appeared to be younger than Brock, walked directly up to him and told him Jade had lost a lot of blood and came dangerously close to needing a transfusion.

"Is she going to be okay?" Brock interrupted.

"She's weak and on an IV for fluids, but yes, she will pull through." Brock sighed in relief and moved his stained fingers through his long bangs. "We ran some tests to find the cause of her acute bleeding," the doctor continued to explain. "We looked at her blood count for anemia, and we also ruled out uterine lesions through an ultrasound. We discovered that your wife," Brock didn't correct the doctor, "had an ectopic pregnancy." Brock's eyes widened. Jade was pregnant. And he didn't know what the word ectopic meant. "The embryo attached itself outside of the uterus. The baby didn't survive. The damage to that particular fallopian tube is excessive, and the other isn't in capable shape. I'm sorry, it's unlikely that she will ever be able to have children," the doctor added.

"I want to see her," Brock said, unsure of how he should feel. This was too much information at once. All he wanted to know was Jade had survived that horrific ordeal. Instead, he stood there, hearing he and Jade had created a baby, and probably would never be able to again. He forced himself to think of how he only wanted her to live. And his prayer had been answered.

When he walked into her hospital room, Jade was alone. She looked so still, lying there in bed, hooked up to an IV, and her eyes were closed on such a pale face. Brock's heart went out to her. She had come to mean so much to him in so little time. And, tonight, she could have been taken away. Just like that. He could have lost her.

Brock sat down beside the bed, and took her hand in his. She stirred as he brought her fingers to his lips. Her eyes opened and she formed a faint smile for him.

"You scared the hell out of me, little lady," Brock said, keeping his voice quiet.

"Me, too," Jade responded. "I still don't know what happened, exactly. I tried asking the doctor earlier but I couldn't stay awake long enough for his full explanation." Her voice sounded terribly weak as she spoke to him. Brock had no idea how Jade was going to feel about knowing she was pregnant, but he was relieved to be the one to tell her rather than some stranger wearing a white lab coat.

"You had what is called an ectopic pregnancy," Brock began to explain. "The baby can't survive that way, out of the uterus. And, the doctor said you have damage to both of your fallopian tubes, so it's unlikely you will be able to have another baby." Brock wanted to be sure to say *another* because Jade did have a baby, and she still could change her mind about raising her.

Jade was silent for a long while. Brock thought she would fall back to sleep, but then she finally spoke to him. "Funny how life works, isn't it? I'm moving on from my past, from a baby who I honestly feel is better off without me. You still have hurt in your eyes from a lie that tore apart your plans to become a daddy. Both of us pretty much admitted it would be okay if we didn't have babies. We only need each other. The entire time we were setting the stage for our future, we had no idea we had created a baby. A baby that didn't stand a chance from the beginning." As Jade was rambling, Brock was trying to read her. Was she upset? Relieved? "I guess this is God's way of trying to tell us, me especially, that if I can't own up to the baby he already gave me, there will be no more."

"Jade," Brock interrupted her, "no one is being punished here." She squeezed his hand.

"I need time to think," she told him.

"Of course you do," Brock responded.

"When can I go home?" she asked.

"We have to see what the doctor says about how soon you will be able to travel." Brock was going to call his father and tell him to send another foreman to the Base in O'Fallon. He needed to focus on taking care of Jade right now.

"I meant, your house," Jade clarified, and Brock smiled at her. She already thought of his home as theirs.

***

An hour later, Jade was resting when Brock walked out of her hospital room, down the hallway, and into the waiting lounge to call his father. He told him what had happened to Jade, not the specifics about the pregnancy or her female issues, just how she had lost a lot of blood and would be hospitalized for a little while until she regained her strength. Brock was adamant about not leaving her side, and not being able to return to the construction site on the military Base in O'Fallon. His father understood, and told him not to worry about anything except for taking care of the woman he loved.

***

Instead of being in Tennessee for the weekend, Jade and Brock ended up staying for a week. They arrived back in O'Fallon, at their hotel, one week to the day that Jade had been hospitalized.

It took a few days in Tennessee for Jade to regain her complete strength, but once she did, she bounced back quickly. Brock worked very little at his office headquarters, because he wanted to keep his eyes on Jade. He was still shaken from what had happened. They spoke at length about finding out they were pregnant, and what that would have meant for them. Jade was thinking about their conversation as she sat alone in the hotel room, with the custody papers in front of her. She was positioned on the bed, with her back up against the headboard and her knees pulled up to her chest. The papers were beside her on the duvet. The annulment document was already signed. She was planning to return it to Rhett today. She had the choice to return that one only, and tear up the papers which would cease her parental rights to Aspen. Jade remembered Angie warning her not to sign those papers. She didn't have to sign them. And then there was that conversation she had with Brock after her health scare because she had been pregnant. Even though the baby did not survive, and definitely could not have, Jade's mind was flooded with *what ifs*.

"Be honest with me," she remembered Brock saying to her as they laid by the pool together. "How would you have felt, what would you have done if you would have had a healthy pregnancy?"

Jade thought for a moment before she replied. "I would have been scared out of my mind to go down that road again," she answered. "After giving birth, becoming a mom is supposed to happen so naturally. It's expected to be flawless, or at least it seems that way. Here is your baby, love her forever, unconditionally. A woman is expected to fall in love with her baby, a part of her she would carry in her arms for awhile and then always in her heart. That did not happen to me. I tried it once, and I failed. I lost myself in the process and you were the one who eventually came along and helped me, you saved me in so many ways. I don't think, aside from the female complications I now have, I could ever give you a child because the risk is entirely too great. I could lose you."

It was Brock's turn to be silent for awhile and, finally, he spoke. "I've never been one to look too far ahead and plan for anything, because you just never know how life will go," he began. "I grew up an only child and I was always looking for companionship. When my parents were busy, I wanted a friend over. As I got older, I wanted a life partner. I wanted a woman by my side. I probably pushed too hard sometimes, maybe even used my money to buy happiness, or to sustain a relationship. And then I learned, firsthand, what it felt like to be used. Pamela hurt me in the worst way. I was alone for almost a year before I met you, and when I did, I knew you were the one I wanted by my side." Jade smiled at him, and he couldn't see the tears in her eyes behind her large, dark sunglasses. "You're not going to lose me. Just be with me, love me. I'm not asking you for anything else."

Jade smiled again, remembering his words. She was a lucky girl to have won Brock Green's heart.

And then there was his mother. Once she and Brock moved to Tennessee permanently, Jade knew she would dealing with more of Karla Green. At work, and in her personal life. Jade was ready to begin a new career at Green Construction, and she only hoped she would be good enough for Brock in his mother's eyes.

Karla had stopped by the house to see Jade when she was recovering. She had been in the gazebo on the grounds, reading a book and sipping a glass of wine. Brock had gone to the office, and Karla had intentionally left then to catch Jade alone.

Jade saw her walking from a distance. A well put together woman for sure. That particular day, she was wearing a straight yellow skirt, close to three inches above the knees, with a white, silk tank top and white chunky-heeled sandals. She looked elegant and Jade assumed she had a matching jacket of some sort which she had taken off when she left the air conditioned office. Jade was relieved at the moment for selecting a cute, little, sage green sundress from her closet today. She did feel intimated by this woman.

Jade had no shoes on inside the gazebo as a pair of white flip flops lay on the floor board beside her polished blue toes. "Hello dear, how are you feeling?" Karla asked as she stepped up and inside the gazebo with Jade. She sat down, crossing her legs gracefully, and Jade smiled at her.

"I'm well, thank you," Jade said. "I wish I could offer you a glass," she added, referring to her wine.

"Not before dinner for me, but thank you," Karla said, appearing as if she had something on her mind. And then she started the conversation she had come there to have with Jade.

"Brock told me how frightening it was for you both to wake up in the middle of the night to all of that blood," Karla began. "He also said the hemorrhaging was caused by an ectopic pregnancy." Jade was watching Karla's eyes. She saw sorrow, mostly likely because that embryo which positioned itself outside of Jade's uterus was Karla Green's grandchild. She also could see a spark, maybe just a hint, of excitement in her eyes and her expression. Jade assumed Karla now believed she and her son were trying to conceive, or at least not doing anything to prevent it from happening. That was not the case. Unplanned pregnancy happened to Jade before, with Aspen. She had gotten pregnant while on the pill, and now it had occurred again.

"Yes, and that was a complete shock to us," Jade said, trying to vaguely clarify how she and Brock were not, and are not, trying to have a baby.

"Oh I understand," Karla said, but she didn't really. "It would be nice to be married first." *Oh dear Lord*, Jade thought, *this woman was beginning to push.* Her true self, overbearing self, was surfacing.

Jade didn't say anything in response. Yes, she wanted to marry Brock, one day. *But, geez, allow the man to propose first!* But, no, she did not want to have his babies.

"I want to thank you again for offering me the job at your company, and I'd like to be clear that I will accept it when Brock and I return here to live in a couple of months," Jade changed the subject. But, she was being sincere. And she felt grateful.

"I was hoping for that!" Karla exclaimed, clapping her hands together and Jade smiled at her. "Clay and I are very excited to have you on board, and not just in the company. Brock loves you, and seeing him so happy makes his father and

I over the moon with joy. I cannot wait to call you my daughter-in-law. You will want for nothing, and all we want are grandbabies to spoil." Karla was beaming and Jade tried with everything she had not to show an inkling of hesitation or uncertainty in her own eyes and facial expression.

Afterward, Jade told Brock about their conversation and he just shook his head, and said, "That's how she is, and that's why I never told her about Aspen or anything further regarding your reproductive system." The two of them ended up laughing at his comment. His words just sounded funny. They didn't care what anyone else thought. Their lives were their own. Their life together was going to be wonderful.

***

Rhett replied to Jade's text when she notified him that she was ready to deliver the papers. She never mentioned that she had been out of town. Angie was the only one she told that she and Brock had taken a trip back to his home in Tennessee, but Jade never informed her of what happened while they were there. She didn't want to alarm her, and planned to tell her in person now that she was alright again. Jade asked Rhett to meet her. He again suggested the house they used to share, and asked her to be there during his lunch break.

As she drove down Smiley Street, it felt good to be among familiar surroundings again. There was so much Jade knew she would not miss about her hometown, but the few things which did tug at her heartstrings she would just have to tuck into her memory. She saw Rhett's truck parked on the driveway and she pulled her Jeep adjacent to it.

After one knock, Rhett opened the front door. She resisted rolling her eyes. Just the sight alone of seeing him in his red uniform shirt with blue jeans sent her back to the time in her life, not too long ago, when she was miserable.

"Hi, you look nice," he said as he sized her up in another new sundress. This one was pale pink and she wore her dark brown ankle wrap sandals with it, baring her toe nails which were polished to match her dress. Her hair was in a high bun and Rhett stared longer than he knew he should have.

"Thank you," she replied, walking into the house. It never occurred to her this time that the baby could have been there until she saw her empty swing in the living room. It just didn't matter to Jade. Being in that house hardly fazed her this time. And, today, was going to be her last time to come there.

She handed Rhett the signed annulment papers. He took them from her. He flipped through a few pages to find her signature. And then he looked up at her. "No more marriage for us," he said, and she remained silent. "What about the custody papers? They're not here."

Jade didn't hesitate to answer. "No deal on that, Rhett."

"What do you mean, no deal? You wanted out, you haven't been around or involved for weeks now. It really would be no different for you to legally give her up, now would it?"

"She's yours, Rhett. Leave it at that." Jade started to walk away, toward the living room door. She had to get out of there. She wanted to be free of her old life. Completely free. But, on her terms.

Jade thought this meeting was adjourned. Rhett looked angry, or maybe more disappointed, and he didn't have anything else to say. Jade's hand was on the doorknob and she was walking away. And then from the corner of her eye, she saw movement in the kitchen doorway. The neighbor girl whom she used to pay to babysit had come inside of the house from the kitchen entrance and on her hip was Aspen.

Her blonde curly hair was growing out enough to put it up in a short, sprouty ponytail on top of her head. She was wearing a little red eye-lit dress with bright white walking shoes, high enough to cover her small ankles. Nine and a half months seemed early to be walking, but Jade had no idea if Aspen was or not. Jade had never before put shoes on her feet. The baby's eyes were bright and her smile wide. She still had so much drool coming from her mouth with her fist in it as she cooed. She always did love her daddy and right now she was focused on him. It was easier that way, Jade thought to herself. Easier than if her baby girl was looking at her. Sad to see her. Happy to see her. Any reaction from Aspen right now just may have broken Jade.

The babysitter said nothing as Rhett walked over to her and took Aspen from her arms. He continued to walk in Jade's direction and he stopped very close to her. Jade never looked at him, only at the baby. She was beautiful. And happy. And no longer hers. "Say goodbye to mommy," Rhett said keeping his eyes fixed on Jade's. He wanted to cause her pain now. He hated her for what she did to him, and to their family.

Jade never said anything to him, or in response to his cruel comment. Maybe, after everything, she deserved it. She deserved to feel sad to see her baby girl again. If she was sad, she didn't let the emotion linger. She just opened the door, walked out, and left it wide open behind her. *Rhett can close the door*, she thought, *I've had enough closure to last me a lifetime.*

Chapter 17

Jade drove directly to her grandmother's house. In less than five minutes, she was pulling onto the driveway in her red Jeep, near the detached garage. Angie wasn't outside, so Jade rang her doorbell before letting herself in. She knew she was welcome to walk in, but she always gave her a notice by ringing the bell prior.

Angie came around the corner quickly from the kitchen with a combined look of surprise and sheer happiness. "Jadey! You're home!" Jade fell into her arms and Angie made a point to hold her especially close and tight.

"I've missed you, Gram," Jade said, eventually pulling out of her arms.

"Not as much as I've missed you," Angie said, as the two of them walked into her kitchen and sat down at the table together. "Can I get you a drink or something to eat?"

"No, Gram. All I need is you and your listening ears," Jade said, smiling, "and boy do I have a lot to tell you."

Jade proceeded to tell Angie all about Brock Green's life in Franklin, Tennessee. She described, in vivid detail, his home, his land, his business, and his parents. Angie was in awe of how much this man had to offer her granddaughter. She knew Jade enjoyed the finer things in life, especially lately, but she had no idea the extent of it all. Until now.

"So why did a weekend getaway turn into a week-long trip?" Angie asked, knowing Brock had work to complete in O'Fallon before he and Jade moved permanently to his home in Tennessee.

"That was out of our control, Gram," Jade told her. "I ended up in the hospital and needed a few days to recover before traveling."

"Jadey...you didn't tell me. What happened to you?" Angie looked at her, long and hard, and saw nothing different, and certainly nothing alarming.

"I woke up hemorrhaging, it was awful, Gram," Jade began to explain. "I thought I was going to die, and I scared Brock so badly. He's still being overprotective with me." Jade smiled and Angie wore a look of worry on her face. "The doctor discovered why I was bleeding from my reproductive system. I had an ectopic pregnancy. After a series of tests, they concluded my fallopian tubes are now useless. No more babies for me."

The first and only thing Angie thought of was Aspen. And she hoped her granddaughter had done the same the moment she received the grim news from the doctor. *Run to your baby. Hold her. And never let her go again.*

"I think God is sending you a message, Jadey. Grasp what you've been given. Aspen is a blessing. Realize that before it's too late." Angie tried not to lecture Jade. She had missed her so much while she was away, but now she wanted her to see what was right in front of her.

"You're not saying anything I haven't already thought of, or confided in Brock about," Jade said, "but nothing's changed for me, Gram."

Angie shook her head. "Take more time to process this. Be absolutely sure of what you're doing."

"I am, and Brock is as well. He knows me, inside and out, and he wants to spend the rest of his life with me. I want that, too, without Rhett's baby."

"She's your baby, too!" Angie exclaimed, raising her voice, hoping a tone equivalent to yelling would get through to Jade.

"Not anymore," Jade replied. "I just came from the house. I gave Rhett the annulment papers."

"Do not tell me you also signed the custody papers!" Angie was trying to keep herself from becoming completely livid.

"No, I did not, Gram," Jade answered, and then she paused. "She was there. I saw Aspen. She has her daddy to take very good care of her. This is what I want."

"Jadey, listen, you could offer her a different life now. You're happy, you're in love. You have what it takes to provide for your baby now." Angie didn't mean that money could alter everything for the better, but she knew it certainly could help.

"I recognize that," Jade said, "but it doesn't change anything. I am still the person I was before. I can't be a mother. I don't ever want to be a mother." Angie momentarily closed her eyes, realizing she was fighting a losing battle. She needed to stop and just listen again to Jade.

"Tell me about your health, are you completely recovered?" Angie asked her.

"Pretty much, yes," Jade said.

"Follow up with your doctor here, before you move," Angie suggested. "Change your birth control so you can avoid another ordeal like you just went through."

"I've already changed pills, and I will be fine, Gram. It was just an eye-opener for me. None of us know how long we're here. We just need to seize every moment, and be happy." Angie wished that horrific experience would have opened Jade's eyes to Aspen more than likely being the only child she will ever be able to give birth to. She wished Jade would want to seize every moment with her.

***

Two months later, Jade turned in the key card for their hotel suite. She told the front desk clerk to charge their remaining bill to Brock's credit card. After six months, he was checking out of that hotel and going home. And he was taking Jade with him. Brock was outside in the parking lot, loading up the last of their things into his truck. He had already made arrangements for Jade's Jeep to be sent to their home in

148

Franklin. He always went the extra mile for her. He wanted to make her happy. And she was.

Jade was quiet as they drove out of town, the town she grew up in. As they exited onto Interstate 64, she thought of the goodbyes. Her goodbye to her mother wasn't emotional, but it was more heartfelt than Jade had expected. Sher told her how she was making herself a permanent and regular fixture in Aspen's life, how she felt like a real grandmother now, and she reassured Jade that she was going to make up for lost time and past mistakes. Jade understood what she meant. Sher wasn't the best, most supportive, loving mother. She never tried to be, and that was the problem. When Sher put her heart into something, she excelled. Jade felt oddly comforted knowing Aspen would get to know her, and love her. And Jade never said a word when Sher told her she will have pictures of Aspen, and stories to tell, if Jade ever wanted her to share. All she had to do was ask.

Telling Angie goodbye was ten times more difficult. Jade had loved and lost in her young life, but the one constant had always been *her Gram*. Five hours, three hundred miles, was not too awfully far away. But, it wasn't a hop, skip, and a jump away either. They talked about the life Jade was moving toward, they hugged, held hands, and all the while Angie remained strong for Jade. As always.

"You live your life how you see fit. Do what makes you happy. I understand you, completely. I always have, and I always will. I expect to hear from you often, and I foresee a road trip in my near future if you have room to accommodate me for a few days." Jade smiled at Angie before she hugged her tight one last time, and wholeheartedly agreed to everything she asked, before she told her goodbye. *For now.* Jade was crying, and Angie smiled sweetly at her, wiping away the tears on her cheeks as if she were four years old again and had skinned her knee. A skinned knee was so much easier to patch up. There was no patching up what Jade was doing now, and Angie knew all too well how that felt. And so she reminded her again how it will never be too late to come back. "No matter what, you can always come home again," Angie said, making Jade look directly into her eyes. "A change of heart happens."

Jade smiled to herself and blinked back the tears in her eyes as the truck wheels took her mile after mile, away from her old life to her new. She kept thinking about her grandmother and how strong she was throughout her entire life. She wanted to be just like her, and in so many ways, she already was.

Chapter 18

Other than her clothes, and she did have a lot more since Brock had encouraged her to use his credit card to treat herself regularly, Jade didn't have all that much to unpack once she moved in to Brock's home in Franklin. She settled in quickly over the weekend they moved, and she was ready to start her new job on Monday.

Brock left the house an hour before Jade. She was standing inside their walk-in closet, half naked in her white lace bra and matching panties, where all of her clothing and shoes were on one side and Brock's on the other. She had already tried on four outfits, two dresses and two skirts, and she still felt indecisive about what to wear on the first day of her new job. She was nervous and excited, too. This was her new life and she wanted to make a good impression at the office today. Life with Brock was easy. He loved and accepted her for who she was. Their relationship felt effortless. Starting a job, which could possibly turn into a career, was new for Jade. Would she be smart enough? *Of course she was*, she told herself. What she didn't know, she would learn. It was that simple. Everyone had to start somewhere. Jade hurried to slip into a peach-colored suit. The skirt was about the length, two or three inches above her knee, as she had seen Karla wear. The short jacket, which matched the skirt, had three-quarter-length sleeves, and she wore a white scoop neck silk blouse with cap sleeves underneath. It was very business-like, and so unlike Jade. But, it seemed appropriate for her first day. She slipped into her open-toe nude heels and walked out of the door. She kept the windows up and the top closed on the Jeep, not wanting to mess up her hair, perched on top of her head in a high bun.

Brock had driven her to the office over the weekend so she would know exactly how to get there on her own. He showed her around, too, when no one else was there. Jade already knew where she would be working, the location of her desk and all.

The first person Jade saw when she walked in was a young woman, probably around her age, and she wore a warm, inviting smile on her face. Her clothes were nice, but inexpensive looking. Jade noticed the short powder blue linen dress with cap sleeves and taupe pointed-toe heels, which sounded hollow on the hardwood floor in the office, a sign of a cheap shoe. Jade, knowing how pricey her suit was, immediately wondered if she had overdressed, or dressed too flashy. *Better than being underdressed,* she thought to herself, as the woman introduced herself as Dinah.

"You must be Jade," Dinah said, again warmly. "I will show you to your office."

"Office?" Jade asked. She thought her desk was in the main, open front office, with three or four others. She followed Dinah through a long hallway and then stopped as she did in front of an open office door. Jade looked inside. The space was immense. The entire back wall of the cooperate office, behind her desk, was windows. It was incredibly bright in there, everything was white, the flooring, the walls and then there was the ritzy decor, all in black. The desk. The chairs. The framed pictures on the walls. The window trim. "This is my office?" Jade questioned Dinah again.

"Yes, aren't you lucky? Mrs. Green wanted some changes made. Her office is now yours." Dinah had no idea if Jade had worked her way up the ladder in other construction firms and was deserving of this fancy new title and job, but she had her suspicions about her. She didn't seem comfortable in a cooperate atmosphere. And Dinah had also heard she was living with the vice president, Brock Green. Again, lucky her, Dinah sneered to herself. She had been crushing on Brock for five years. She never was able to catch his eye. He pretty much patted her on top of the head when she flirted, complimented him, batted her eyes, or wore tighter clothes, higher heels. It was as if she was next of kin in his eyes, or a wallflower. That would explain why she was stationed in the main office and making thirty thousand dollars a year compared to this woman who had already been invited to take over the bosses office and be handed a fancy new title. Dinah's warm smile was fake. Behind it, she hated the world and especially women like Jade who had the world by the ass. Or so she assumed. "I will leave you to settle in. Mrs. Green is conducting a board meeting," Dinah stretched out her arm and pointed out of the office door and catty-cornered across the hall. Jade noticed more windows, this time to a conference room, and she could see Karla in a black suit with another skirt the length of her own today. She was standing up, in front of a long, rectangular table full of business people, both men and women. Jade wanted to take a closer look, but Dinah spoke again and stole her attention back. "The meeting will be over shortly. Just wait in here for Mrs. Green."

When Dinah exited the office, she left the door wide open. Jade couldn't resist walking toward the doorway and stood there as she watched the meeting from a distance, through the window. Karla Green had a way about her. She, like her son, knew how to capture a room. Jade's eyes searched the people seated at that table. She saw men in suits, women in skirts and business wear, and then she saw Clay Green and his son, seated side by side. They were in jeans, starched long-sleeved shirts and boots, but no hats. They weren't the suit and tie type, and it was their company so their attire was their choice. Clay was more laidback than Brock, even shy to some extent. Brock may have looked like his father, in physical appearance and style, but his business intellect was his mother's and he, like her, didn't mind the stares in public, or even the girls falling all over him. Jade had teased him about that. She noticed the waitresses who flirted with him when they dined out, she saw the double-takes from other women when they were anywhere in public. Brock only laughed, and reminded her he was taken. And she was all he wanted.

As Jade was watching Karla, the way she carried herself, the seriousness on her face as she spoke business lingo, and pointed a time or two to the overhead view on PowerPoint, or Excel, or whatever people used now. Jade had a lot to learn. And she was ready to learn it. The meeting appeared to adjourn as the people seated at the table began to stand up, some in unison and others lagging. That is when Jade saw Karla catch her eye, and she held her stare and broke into a welcoming smile. Jade waved, slightly, she didn't want to seem too eager, or school-girl like. And then she left the door open and walked back into the office which was hard to believe was hers.

Moments later, Karla walked in.

Jade had been standing near the window, which spanned the entire back wall of the office, looking out at the view. It was a downtown business view with such a vibrant blend of historic preservation and modern sophistication. Some of the buildings on Main Street had structures which resembled churches. There were antique shops, brick-and-mortar gift and book stores, fashion-forward boutiques, privately owned art galleries. Jade already saw this town as an eclectic community whose locals have never met a stranger. And she was looking at the woman who had made her feel most at home.

Karla walked over to her and embraced her, warmly. "Welcome to your new office, honey, I hope you like it," she said, sounding more southern than Jade had ever noticed.

"It's unbelievable," Jade said, wanting to add, *and I heard it was yours,* but she held back. "I'm not sure I deserve this kind of extravagance. I haven't even started working for you yet."

Karla smiled. "I thought about giving you a secretarial position for which you could be trained for those things you are not familiar with like the industry's specialized knowledge, the jargon and acronyms. You would work in the office setting or on jobsites in one of our office trailers, which would make you a field administrator," Karla explained, and Jade didn't think either one of those positions sounded unflattering. "You will be doing clerical duties here and there like filing bid documents, contracts, subcontracts, and purchase orders. Project foremen and superintendents may keep a daily project diary that you will be responsible for maintaining. Every company has different needs, our staff is sizable so there are meetings to schedule, a staff calendar to maintain. It all gets done. We have added you to our staff to help us continue to thrive, not to dump it all on you the first day and overwhelm you," Karla said, attempting to reassure Jade.

"I understand, and I'm ready to contribute all I can to your company, Mrs. Green," Jade responded, sincerely, but she still didn't understand why she had to perform clerical duties in the bosses' extravagant office.

"Call me, Karla, and I will call you our new executive director."

Jade's eyes widened. She was not qualified to hold such a title. If this woman, president and co-owner of Green Construction, only knew she had a high school diploma and bartending experience, she would never be standing there offering her a prominent title, let alone her office. "You can't be serious!" Jade said, not believing how her life had changed. Drastically, for the better.

"I'm as serious as my son is about having you in his life," Karla replied. "No one has ever had the effect on him as you do. He's happy, and I want to keep him that way."

"So you're doing this for me, but not really, because it's for Brock?" Jade was being forthright, almost too much so, right now.

Karla smiled at her again. "You are quite a woman. I like how direct you are. If you're thinking it, you say it. It's my motto, too."

"It gets me into trouble sometimes," Jade confessed with a crooked smile.

"Me too," Karla giggled, "but look around you, it's also made me a very successful woman. This used to be my office, it's yours now, Jade. I moved to Clay's office because he's never here for more than meetings. He's still the kind of man who wants to be out there swinging a hammer alongside of his crew. And Brock is very much the same."

"I will do my best not to disappoint you as I learn the trade," Jade said to her.

"You won't disappoint me," Karla said. "I have reliable office staff to answer the phones when our clients call, and see to it that the important documents get filed. The success of this business is not in your hands. In fact, you can pop in and out of here anytime you wish for a mani-pedi or retail therapy. Just keep my son happy and you and I will have a sweet deal."

Jade felt uneasy, and quite frankly, used. "So you're telling me that I'm being given a fancy title and who knows how much money, just to show up here? No work needs to be done? Oh wait, the job that is expected of me is to keep the man I love happy? Am I not already doing that without a paycheck from Green Construction?" Jade felt miffed now.

"You're overreacting, Jade. The big picture is you are, or will soon be, a part of our family and we have titles and prestige and integrity and you will, too." The business tone was back in Karla's voice.

"I only wanted to work for you, to feel the self-worth which comes with having a job, or a career, where I could feel like I was contributing and making a difference," Jade said, standing tall beside a woman who continued to greatly intimidate her.

"In due time, that will come," Karla replied. "For now, accept this position with grace, and do what you're told to do." Jade felt chilled. This woman was not to be messed with.

"I do accept all you have offered to me and given me already," Jade replied, reminding herself with every word to bite her tongue if needed. *Be nice, Jade. This woman could one day be your mother-in-law.* "And I do appreciate it all, Karla. But, you must know that I love your son, regardless. In fact, I could be just as happy tending bar down here on Main Street." Jade said, purposely, just to see Karla's reaction.

First, she laughed. A real laugh, a loud and deep down from the pit of her stomach kind of laugh, and then she grew serious. "Never say that. You will be a Green one day, and we are not losers."

A loser. Jade was still thinking about Karla's statement hours later as she sat alone in that big, fancy office bored out of her mind.

Chapter 19

Jade made it home only about thirty minutes before Brock. She was happy to take off her business wear and slip into a cute little sundress, this one was coral colored. Brock had texted her, midday, and told her he was taking her out to dinner to one of his favorite restaurants downtown to celebrate her first day at Green Construction. Jade had not seen him at the office, only through the window while the board meeting was taking place. She missed him and was ready to unwind for the evening. She told herself not to complain to him about her boring day, and she also decided against telling him about the conversation with his mother. Not yet anyway. She just wanted to enjoy herself tonight.

When Brock walked into their bedroom, Jade was slipping into wheat-colored wedges in front of a full-length floor mirror. "Keep dressing like that after a long, hard day of work and I will want to take you out and show you off every night," Brock stated, as she walked toward her and pulled her into a kiss.

"You look good enough to show off, too," she said, smiling.

"Just good enough?" he asked her, giggling, and she laughed too. And then he inquired about her day.

"It was all good," she said, putting on her sincerest face, "and I think it will only get better." She hoped, but wondered if that was a lost cause.

***

Brock drove her to the historic factory, a popular complex in Franklin for entertainment, shopping and dining. He introduced her to Saffire, a restaurant and bar with an intimate, urban feel. Jade loved the atmosphere and Brock raved about everything on the menu. He frequented there often. Jade decided on the pan-roasted salmon and Brock chose the blackened fish tacos. When their waitress brought her white wine and Brock's beer, Jade took one sip and then excused herself to use the ladies room. She drank an entire bottle of water before they left for the restaurant, it was something she had trained herself to do before every meal to prevent herself from overeating. And, now, she needed to empty her bladder before dinner.

As she walked through the restaurant toward the ladies restroom, she passed the bar. She glanced at the middle-aged man, with specs of gray in his dark hair, tending bar and that's when she thought back to all of her nights at Shooters. She was a different person then, for sure. She had led a different life, far different than now.

Her eyes moved to a sign behind the bar, advertising help wanted from eleven a.m. to seven p.m. Jade's first thought was she should apply. And then she retracted that thought. She had a new life now. Why would she want to revert back to a part of her old one?

***

Being out on the town, for dinner, to shop, or for the nightlife was quite the life for Jade. She had gone from rags to riches as she was well aware and did not take any of it for granted. She loved Brock. She did not miss her old life. Jade should have felt ashamed, but she didn't miss her baby either. The only thing she was second guessing was accepting Karla's job offer at Green Construction. By Friday of her first week as executive director, she had not done more than surf the Internet in her spacious cooperate office, and attend a few meetings alongside Karla so she could be introduced to the board members and look the part in front of her co-workers. Jade refrained from complaining, or standing up to, Karla. Still, it didn't feel right to Jade to be paid a six-figure salary to do nothing but *look the part*.

Jade thought about telling Brock what was going on, especially since an entire work week had gone by and nothing had changed. Jade deserved better than that. She had something to offer the company and she was not being given a chance to even try.

A few from the office crew, Dinah included, had invited Jade to go out for lunch with them at the end of the week. They were going to Saffire and Jade didn't hesitate to join them. She loved the atmosphere there, and thoroughly enjoyed the food.

The restaurant was within walking distance, but the skies looked threatening. It had been raining for two days and there was a seventy percent chance for more rain. One of the guys at the office drove four others, including Jade, there.

Everyone was nice, and Jade was having a good time getting to know a few of her coworkers. She was trying especially hard to learn, and remember, all of their names.

Jade ordered a crab cake salad and she drank two glasses of iced water with lemon before their lunch was brought to the table. Once again, she needed to empty her bladder before the meal, so she left the table and made her way past the bar.

The help wanted sign was still there. They needed a daytime into early evening bartender. Jade watched the middle-aged man behind the bar. A customer had just walked up to the corner of the bar, and Jade thought he looked to be about her grandmother's age. He was dapper in what she guessed was his seventies and Jade smiled to herself when she thought of how she wished Angie would have a companion. She was still very much a beautiful woman. *I'll have whatever is on draft,* Jade heard him say, *and an old fashioned for my wife.*

Jade giggled to herself. *How many times hadn't she mixed that drink for the regulars at Shooters!* She still had not walked past the bar and came to a stop when the bartender said he had no idea how to make an old fashioned. *Never heard of it, sir,* he said, *but if you tell me what's in it, I will surely mix it up for your wife.* The older man shrugged his shoulders, *I don't have the slightest idea. I'm an uncomplicated man, gimme a beer and I'm happy.* The two men laughed in unison and Jade stepped up to them.

"Simple syrup, bitters, ice cubes and add whiskey. Garnish with an orange slice and a cocktail cherry," Jade spoke to the bartender with confidence and a sweet smile. The older gentleman stepped back and nodded his head and said, "Sounds good to me," and the bartender hesitated for a moment. "Are you serious? Come on back here and make that drink, sweetheart."

Jade didn't hesitate after she laughed out loud. She walked behind the bar, the bartender handed her a glass and she went to work. She found the bitter selection and chose an orange flavored one. She combined a generous squirt of sugar syrup and stirred it about a dozen times before she filled the glass with iced cubes and then added the rest whiskey, stirring again until the drink was cold and the alcoholic bite softened. Then, Jade garnished the drink with a cherry, swizzle stick, and straw.

She served it to the older gentleman and the bartender accepted his money, *with a tip for the beautiful young lady.* The bartender turned to Jade afterward and spoke. He was only about a half an inch taller than Jade in her heels and he nearly looked her square in the eye when he said, "I'm Josh, I own this place and I haven't been able to find a decent bartender to save my life, until today. So, the job is yours. Please tell me you'll accept." Jade laughed out loud again. She was having fun with this flattery. Saffire was far more upscale than Shooters, but still, Jade was in her element.

Josh had a baby face, but he looked to be in his late forties. His wavy dark hair with specks of gray gave away his age. Jade continued to smile, but she shook her head. "I have a job already, I'm an executive at Green Construction." This was the first time she used her title and she liked it. She liked being *somebody*. But, she hated her job. She was quick to remind herself of that. She was bored there. She was not happy looking the part and not doing a damn thing to feel useful.

"So, quit, and come work for me," Josh said, and before Jade could get a word in edgewise, he spoke to his bar crowd. "Everyone, this beautiful lady has just been hired to tend bar at lunchtime." Cheers erupted with some clapping and whistles in the mix and Jade felt her face flush. "You can't do that, I never said yes!"

"What's your name?" Josh asked, with a mischievous smile.

"Jade, but-"

"Please welcome, Jade!" Josh was relentless and Jade just decided to humor him for a moment. *What would be the harm?* She even remembered some of the signature cocktails from when she read the drink menu while dining there with Brock.

Jade spent the next fifteen minutes mixing and serving drinks. She was in the middle of making A Good Man Is Hard to Find with tequila, hibiscus liqueur, and lime when Dinah from the office was standing directly in front of her, with only the bar separating them. She didn't seem amused as she told

Jade their food was ready and her crab cake salad awaited. "Be right there," Jade told her without further explanation. She didn't owe Dinah anything. She didn't even like her. It had only taken Jade a few days of being in the same office building with her to see through the phony smile and friendly facade.

Jade made eye contact with Josh next and said, "One more and I'm leaving you. My lunch awaits." He grinned, pretended to be tipping his hat to her, and said, "Well it was great fun while it lasted," and then he looked disappointed knowing he still needed a bartender. Jade would have been perfect for Saffire.

Her last order to fill was a Cormac with bourbon, grilled pineapple, and rosemary simple. Jade giggled when a woman, who reminded her in age and personality of her Gram again, told her to double the bourbon because *her hip was bothering her today.*

In the middle of the laughter, Jade had served her last drink and she stood there taking in the feeling of this. The lights were low above the bar. The crowd was happy, loopy too, but happy nonetheless. She could feel herself smiling as she turned to walk away, back to her table of boring cooperate office people, and that's when she looked up and directly at Karla Green, standing toe to toe with her.

"What are you doing?" Karla asked her through clenched teeth. She did not ask what she was doing *there*, at Saffire, she asked what she was *doing*. Brock's mother did not care if Jade was eating lunch. She could eat lunch anywhere she damn well pleased. What Karla cared about and was trying not to be obviously irate about was the fact she had just witnessed the woman in her son's life serving drinks behind a bar. Like, in her words, *losers* do.

Jade eyes widened and then she smiled as if this was no big deal. Because, truly, it was no big deal. "You'll laugh," Jade began, "I was on my way to the ladies room when I overheard the bartender unsure of how to make an old fashioned. I ended up putting my two cents in and making a few drinks while here on my lunch break." Jade pointed to the table across the way with a handful of Green Construction employees, but Karla never turned her head to look.

Karla did not laugh as she did not find any of this *funny*. She was clearly embarrassed. She was not the type of woman to make a scene, but here and now she wanted to get her point across to Jade. Not loudly, though, just clearly.

The two of them walked a short distance away from the bar and stood in a walkway to the kitchen which was currently clear. "I think you know what I just saw is not acceptable," Karla began. "My son-"

"Acceptable for whom?" Jade interrupted. "For all we know, the woman I helped serve an old fashioned to could have been a past client of Green Construction. Your husband and son may have built her mansion on the hill."

Karla shook her head. "That is besides the point!" she raised her voice more than she intended. "Don't ever let me catch you behind a bar, serving anyone! This family, the family my son is very serious about you being a part of, does not do that sort of thing."

Before Jade could respond, Clay walked up behind his wife, put his arm around her lower back and greeted Jade with, "Well, hello, I hope this means you are joining us for lunch." *Us*, as Jade noticed next, also included Brock. He was walking up, behind his father. He looked as if he had gotten caught in the rain. Right now, Jade felt as if she, too, had gotten rained on. More like stormed on. This woman, the love of her life's mother, was someone she wondered if she could tolerate any longer. She didn't want to live up to her expectations. She should not have to. She was her own person. Brock loved her for who she was. It was time Jade came clean with Karla. It was time she knew Jade Connors, in full detail. *The woman who tended bar all night long at a dive. The young wife who didn't want to be married anymore. And, the mother who abandoned her child.*

Chapter 20

Karla was an altogether different person throughout lunch. Her anger appeared to have diminished. Jade explained how she was supposed to be eating her crab cake salad at the table with her coworkers, and Karla said, "I'll take care of it," as she flagged down their waitress and informed her Jade had switched tables and would need a fresh meal, and to bill her table for both. *A woman in charge,* Jade thought. And there was nothing wrong with that. It was admirable to see Karla in control, but Jade was beginning to feel suffocated by her, given how she was now in control of too much of Jade's life.

Lunch, after she had finally eaten, was delicious as they sat near a window and watched it rain. They talked business and they talked about Jade settling in at the house and at work. Brock was attentive to Jade. He wanted to make her feel included and comfortable, but he had no idea how she felt about her new job. Or about his mother.

After they had eaten and paid their bill, the men suggested the ladies wait inside, near the door, while they ran outside in the rain to get the car and pull it closer to the building. Jade and Karla were left standing at the door and no other restaurant patrons were near.

"Forgive me for overreacting, earlier," Karla broke the ice, and Jade thought, *you've got to be kidding me.* "What I should have taken under consideration was you used to be in this element, managing a restaurant. I understand now, you were just trying to help, even if it was behind the bar." Jade wondered why she had to phrase it like that. What's wrong with being *behind the bar?*

"I think what you don't understand is who I am," Jade began, as she could see out the door how Brock and his father had just reached their car and were getting in. "There is so much about me that you do not know. I'm not perfect, but I love your son and I know he loves me."

"It really doesn't matter to me who you were," Karla replied. "Honestly, that may surprise you, but it's true. What matters to me is now, and how you need to act like one of us."

So you would be fine with knowing I used to tend bar in an age-old tavern, downtown O'Fallon, where the pay was awful and the hours were when most women were getting beauty sleep? Would it also not matter to you that I was married, less than a year, and when I left my husband I also left my baby? Jade imagined telling Karla everything, but now was not the time or place. And, she didn't want to disrespect Brock. She needed to speak to him first.

Brock and his father were sitting in the car, directly outside of the door. It was pouring down rain and their windshield wipers were on rapid speed. They assumed the ladies were waiting for the downpour to lessen. When, really, the storm between them was nowhere near calm.

***

The first thing Jade did when she got home a few hours later was pour herself a glass of wine. She sat down on the pale yellow sofa in the living room with twenty-two-foot-high ceilings. She was barefoot and her legs were curled up underneath her as she sunk comfortably into the large couch cushion while still wearing a short black skirt and sleeveless red blouse from the work day. And then Brock walked in.

He slipped off his wet boots at the door as it was still raining outside, and he walked over to her and sat down. "Home sweet home. I'm so glad it's the weekend. I haven't seen enough of you this week," he said rubbing her bare knee with his entire hand.

"We just had lunch together today," she giggled.

"I didn't have you all to myself though, so that doesn't count," he smiled. "While we are on the subject, how's it going between you and my mother?"

Jade wondered why he asked. Karla had done a perfect job of pretending she had not been upset all throughout lunch. "I admire your mother for her business sense. She really has it together," Jade answered, carefully. The last thing she wanted to do was bash his mother. Brock was close to her. He was her only son. Her baby. So, Jade didn't know how to approach the topic of his mother. She certainly had issues with the woman, issues that were mounting.

"But?" Brock asked her. "I hear hesitation in your voice. Talk to me, babe. Did she say something to upset you?"

"Tell me something about your mother," Jade began. "Does she have a history of meddling in your relationships?"

"Yes," Brock answered and immediately asked, "Why?"

"She wants me in your life, but she wants me to live up to her standards," Jade confessed, and then took a long drink of her wine. "The job, the important title with the outrageous salary, is a joke. She will not put me to work. I'm bored shitless!"

Brock's eyes widened. "You've had a miserable week, day in and day out, and you did not tell me?"

"I didn't want to upset anyone."

"Jade, really? This is me you're talking to. If we are going to share our lives together, we have to be honest about everything." Brock looked concerned, and he didn't like her silence.

"Then you had better pour yourself a glass of wine too, because you're going to need it for what I have to tell you," Jade told him, and then he took her glass from her and helped himself to a generous swig from it.

"I have a real problem with being told that I must act like one of you," Jade began. "I do not have an education beyond high school, I used to tend bar, I used to be a wife and a mother. I have a past."

"And I love you for all you used to be and for all you will be with me, in our future," Brock interrupted her.

"I think it's time your mother knows," she said to him.

"Absolutely not," Brock replied. "It's none of her business."

"She saw me today, at Saffire, I was behind the bar, mixing a drink. Long story, no one knew the recipe, but I did. She was so angry and adamant about how I should never cross the line again. Apparently, I was treading near loser status in her mind."

"She called you a loser?" Brock interjected.

"In a roundabout way, yes."

"I love my mother, but she needs to allow me to live my life, my way."

"Maybe it's time to tell her that, or let me tell her everything and stand back and watch her blow."

"Not a good idea," Brock said, again.

"So what do you suggest I do?" Jade asked him, feeling frustrated. If Brock was a mama's boy, she was going to have her hands full. Jade wanted out of her job, but she didn't want out of their relationship. Not ever. At least she hoped *not ever*. Karla was going to have to be the one to bend, or back off.

"Do what makes you happy, and I hope I'm in that equation," Brock said, leaning forward and kissing her lightly on the lips.

Jade kissed him back. "What if I resign from my job?" Jade was seriously thinking of going back to Saffire. Being behind the bar today made her happy.

"Before you do anything drastic, let me talk to my mother. I can fix this." Jade nodded her head, but she was not in agreement.

"You don't believe me, do you?" Brock asked her, clearly seeing right through her. Jade only smiled at him. "Wait here," was all he said before he left her on the couch and ran up the staircase, skipping every other step in his socks and tight jeans. That was another one of those moments for Jade, watching him, and feeling the deepest gratitude knowing he was hers. It shouldn't have mattered to her that his mother was the most conceited and overbearing person she had ever met.

In mid thought, Brock was coming back. As he descended the stairs, a little slower this time, Jade smiled at him. "What are you up to, Green?"

"You'll see," he responded, landing on the wood flooring and making his way over to her.

"I have a question for you," he said, slowly moving onto one knee at her feet. He was holding a little black velvet box. "I was saving this for a romantic candlelight dinner, or a late night walk on the grounds, where we would end up in the gazebo or the swimming pool, preferably naked," he winked. "But, now, it just feels right."

Tears were welling up in her eyes. This was unexpected, for sure. They had an unspoken understanding or feeling of this being forever, but neither of them had mentioned marriage. Jade, for sure, had not fathomed it, because she had just gotten out of a marriage. An unhappy one.

"Will you marry me, Jade? Be my wife for the rest of our lives together."

"Brock," she said, as the tears spilled over onto her cheeks. "This isn't what I expected. You don't have to act impulsively just because I'm unhappy with your mother."

"Impulsive would be a proposal without a ring. Have you even taken a look at it?" he asked her, and then she moved closer. It was huge. She only had an inexpensive gold wedding band before. She never wore a diamond ring, or diamond anything, in her life. A six-carrot oval-shaped diamond, surrounded by jade stones, was perched on top of a thick gold band. It was stunning. And Jade had no words.

"Can I get a yes here?" Brock asked, smiling.

"What was the question again?" Jade teased, realizing that ring was hers. And so much more. The house. The land. The cars. The bank account. But, Brock Green could have been a man with only the shirt on his back and she would have loved him just the same.

"Be my wife?" Brock asked her again.

"Yes!"

Chapter 21

"Jadey, this is moving too fast." Hearing her grandmother's voice on the phone after she called her to tell her the news was comforting. Even if Angie didn't think rushing into getting engaged was the wisest idea. "The ink is barely dry on your annulment papers."

"I hear you, Gram. I was caught off guard, but it's something I want with all of my heart. You are the one who taught me to live life, seize the moment at hand, before it's too late. I miss you, I hope you know," Jade added, smiling into the phone, but she felt the pang of sadness seep through her.

"I miss you more, Jadey. It helps knowing you're finally happy." Angie refrained from saying how it also hurts knowing days, weeks, months have passed since she left her baby. Aspen was doing well, Angie knew for a fact. Between herself and Sher, they had their share of time with her. Rhett was very good about allowing them to be a regular part of her life, and in turn he needed and appreciated their help. It wasn't easy for him, being a single father, but he was happier no longer living in a rut with Jade. One day, he hoped to remarry and give his baby a mother again.

"I am, minus a glitch or two, but I'm sure everything will work out," Jade said, feeling like it was time to talk to someone, other than Brock, about the woman who was now going to be her future mother-in-law.

"Such as?" Angie asked her.

"Such as Karla Green, my fiancé's mother. She's a little on the overbearing side." *A little*, Jade thought, *more like she defined the term through and through.*

"Most are," Angie replied. "Anything you want to talk about?"

"I'm not thrilled about the job she handed to me, or the way she expects me to act more like *one of them*, her words entirely. She means well, I guess." Jade didn't want to get into too much Karla Green, over the phone. *Maybe time just needed to pass and Brock's mother wouldn't be so bad, after all. Or maybe, hell would freeze over first.*

***

When Brock asked his parents to come over to the house on Saturday, Jade was nervous. She could only imagine how Karla was going to react to the news of their engagement.

First, Karla hugged her son's neck and kissed him on the cheek, and then she turned to Jade, taking both of her hands in her own. "Thank you for making my son so happy, dear. You'll never know how much joy that brings to me and his father." Then, she lifted Jade's left hand up to get a close view of the ring. "Stunning! Simply stunning. Wonderful job, son. Now that's certainly a piece of jewelry to be jealous of." She pulled Jade close and the two of them embraced.

Clay shook his son's hand and then gave him a tight hug as they patted each other hard on the back. And then he was gentle when he hugged Jade. He was a man with a kind heart, just like his son.

"We have so much to plan!" Karla blurted out as the four of them stood together in Brock's immense living room.

"Mom, this is Jade's wedding," Brock said, as Jade smiled at him. "We are going to do what she wants."

"Of course," Karla said, clenching her teeth. "We will compromise on the details." Jade was listening for awhile and then she began to fade. Karla wanted to get started on the guest list immediately. Family. Friends. Business associates. Half the City of Franklin and a quarter of Nashville would be on the guest list. Jade's dress would be made by one of the finest tailors Karla knew. He lived in Paris now and she would fly him in. The list went on and Karla's preferences dominated Jade's.

Two hours later, when Brock's parents left, he turned to her after he closed the door behind them. "You okay?" he asked, knowing how his mother could be and having witnessed Jade's nonchalant reactions to almost everything his mother had brought up and pretty much carved in stone today.

Jade walked over to him. She needed a drink. The four of them had toasted with champagne earlier, but that wasn't enough to wash away the exasperation. She wrapped her arms around his neck and pressed her body, in a cute little white sundress, against his. "Let's elope," she said, in all seriousness.

"Holy Christ, Jade! My mother would kill us." He wanted to giggle, but he was scared to, because he knew Jade was dead serious.

"You said so yourself, this is my wedding," Jade reminded him, purposely giving him a seductive look as she smoothed the palms of her hands over his chest, through his navy blue t-shirt.

"Don't give me that look, Jade. We can't. I'm her only son, only child. It would be just plain cruel to deprive her of giving us a wedding of her–"

"Dreams? *Her* dreams?" Jade interrupted him. "What about what you and I want?"

"All I want is to call you my wife, the sooner the better," he said, kissing her softly on the lips and she responded momentarily before speaking again.

"It will take your mother a year to complete all of those arrangements," Jade complained.

"Then tell her to hurry the hell up. Give her a deadline, but don't take away this once in a lifetime experience for her. Please..."

It was the way he had said it. And it was the way he looked at her. Brock had a heart of gold, and Jade caved. He made her incredibly happy. It was the least she could do for him.

***

The weekend was bliss. The two of them spent their days and nights alone. Much to both of their surprise, Karla left them be after they shared their engagement news. Monday morning came around too soon and as Brock was walking out the door for work, Jade still had not gotten out of bed. She sat up, leaned against the brass headboard, pulling the sheets up to her bare chest. "Do me a favor and tell the boss I will be in late this morning. I want to go for a run first."

"A run?" Brock asked her. He was familiar with her being a gym junkie, but he had never heard her mention running.

"It's something I used to do a lot, and I want to get back into it to keep the gym from getting mundane. I think I'll attempt from here to the nearest park today," she told him.

"That will be four miles round trip. Take it easy, babe. The humidity is high already." Brock worried about her. She felt protected, and loved him even more for it.

"Is there a trail once I get to the park?" Jade asked him.

"There's a paved trail around the park, along the creek,

but it's only about one eighth of a mile," Brock told her. "We should take a walk there tonight, once the sun goes down."

"Sounds nice. Don't forget to tell your mom for me," Jade reminded him as he walked over to the bed and kissed her goodbye.

Jade was quick to get out of bed, wash her face and pull her hair back. She slipped a tight hot pink sports bra over her head and smashed her full breasts into place. She was preparing to run without bounce. She would never forgot what her Gram had taught her in high school, when she made the cross country team. She told her it's important not to cause excessive bounce to your breasts when running because that stretches out the tissue and causes sagging. Jade smiled to herself as she pulled a matching hot pink tank over her bra. She wore tight, short black running shorts and hot pink tennis shoes. All of those clothes were new, too.

Jade started running as soon as she left the estate grounds. Her pace was good and her breathing was steady from the start. It felt good to pound the pavement. The subdivision was beautiful. She looked at the flowers, trees, and landscaping near all of the elaborate homes. She had not been reading street signs, she just remembered from her drives where she needed to turn to make her way to the park.

As she made her second left turn, leaving the final subdivision of homes, Jade caught herself reading the green street sign. She didn't stop running, but her pace changed. Slowed. She was in the Cool Springs area on Aspen Grove Boulevard and the park she was running to was Aspen Grove Park.

Sometimes in life, a song, a person, a place, a scent, something like that, will trigger a memory, an emotion. In this case it was a name. It should not have taken a street sign with her daughter's name displayed on it for Jade to think of her. And maybe even miss her. But, it did.

Jade continued to run, but her mind was no longer in sync with her body. Running now felt useless. Her breathing quickly became rapid, and her side now ached. She slowed to a walk, swinging her arms to move quicker to keep her heart rate up. And then she entered the park, stepping onto the paved path which surrounded a portion of Aspen Grove Park.

The park was fourteen acres and there were three pavilions with charcoal grills, and a large children's playground. Jade looked around as she walked the trail, and then she decided to make her way over toward the playground. There was a red bench there and she wanted to rest for a few minutes. She wanted to chase away her thoughts of Aspen. *She was one year old now. She was probably walking. Talking more. Saying dada, still. She never said mama.*

As Jade sat down on the bench, she glanced around the park and saw two young mothers pushing their little ones side by side on the swings. One child was a girl, and the other a boy. Both appeared to Jade to be about Aspen's age. *Why was she doing this to herself? There was no need to think. No need to compare. No need to go there.*

As Jade was focusing on the swings, another woman, a stocky brunette with her hair up in a ponytail, walked up through the mulch and sat down on the opposite end of the same bench Jade was sitting on. "Hi," the woman said, as Jade was startled..

"Oh, good morning," Jade replied, hoping it was not obvious she had jumped. And then Jade noticed a little boy seated next to her. He was wearing navy blue crocs and the woman, whom Jade assumed was his mother, was taking them off of his feet and shaking out the mulch stuck in them.

Jade smiled at the child who kept talking. "My feet hurt. My mommy is cleaning out my shoes. There's bark in them."

"It's mulch," the woman corrected him.

"My name is Joel," he said to Jade. Again, Jade smiled at him. He had red hair and faint freckles on his fair-skinned face.

"I'm Jade," she said to him. "How old are you, Joel?"

"Two and a half," he answered, proudly, as his mother slipped both of his shoes back on and told him he was free to play. He then ran toward the tunnel slide, after his brief conversation with Jade.

"He's a talker," Jade said to the woman next to her.

"Yes, from early on," she told Jade. The woman paused for a moment, watching her son from a distance, and then she spoke again. "He's my life. Not sure what I'd do without him." *Did she have to say that?* Jade was thinking, *Jesus, I abandoned my child, so apparently I've proved I can live without her.* "Do you have children?" she asked Jade.

"No," Jade answered, too quickly. It was easier to lie.

"Well, just wait, it'll change your life. You'll never be quite the same again. All good, I mean, but suddenly you're wearing your heart outside of your body and you know exactly what it feels like not to give a second thought to laying down your life for another human being." *Holy Christ,* Jade thought, *who is this woman? An angel sent to torture me?*

"Well, your son's a cutie, that's for sure," Jade said, trying to change the subject a tad bit.

"He looks like his daddy," the woman beamed. "I'm not married to him. We were never in a relationship. He visits Joel every so often. Truth be told, I tried to pass off Joel as another man's son." Jade felt like rolling her eyes. This woman was too chatty and revealing way too much personal information.

"Oh," Jade responded.

"My fiancé was loaded. He had the house, cars, pool. His estate is not too far from here." Now Jade's eyes widened. She thought of Brock's story. This woman was Pamela. "I hurt him terribly. He kicked me to the curb. Guess I deserved that," the woman said, laughing out loud. Jade remained silent, but she made friendly eye contact with her. She just didn't want this woman to start asking questions about her. The last thing she was going to tell her was she's now Brock's fiancé. "Just as well that the truth came out," the woman began again. "His mother was a controlling bitch."

It was Jade's turn to laugh out loud. "Oh really?" she asked, knowing there was absolutely no doubt now that this woman was Pamela.

"She was too perfect. Rich. Thin. Beautiful. Successful." She was describing Karla. "She lives the dream, but not many people like her. Probably why she can't sleep at night." Jade gave Pamela a puzzled look. "Insomnia. She was dependant on her prescription medicine." Jade nodded her head and thought how that was something new she had not known about Karla.

Their talk, or more like Pamela's chatter which revealed her past connection to the Greens, was interrupted when Joel called out to his mother. She excused herself from Jade and left to tend to her son.

Jade kept sitting there on the bench. She heard Pamela's words again. *Do you have children? Well, just wait, it'll change your life.* She reached for her cell phone which was strapped to her upper left arm. She held it for a moment, thinking of how the last time she spoke to her mother, before she left town, Sher had told her it would be okay if she wanted to ask about Aspen or see a photograph of her.

No, Jade told herself. She slipped her phone back into the arm band and stood up from the bench. *Maybe just one picture,* she thought again. She sat back down and retrieved her phone again. She found her mother's name in her contact list, and then she pressed the keys to prepare her text message. *Hi. No questions asked. Please. Could you send me a picture?*

Chapter 22

Jade walked back home, took a shower, and got dressed for work. She had not received a response from her text to her mother yet. And the more she thought about how vulnerable she had felt when she sent it, regret began to set in.

She saw the name plate on the door as she entered her office. It read, EXECUTIVE DIRECTOR. That was her, and that was a joke. When Jade placed her handbag on the black leather couch along the wall, she turned to find Karla entering her office.

"You made it in! Brock told me you wanted some time to yourself this morning. Good for you! You will have to do more of that as you plan for the wedding in the coming months!" Jade tried to smile at Karla. She thought about asking her to set the date for them. She was taking charge of everything else, thus far.

"Brock and I want to get married sooner, rather than later," Jade said, making full-on eye contact with Karla. She wasn't as intimated by her as she used to be. Maybe it had something to do with knowing Brock was on her side, and not his mother's.

"Of course. We can make it happen," Karla agreed. "Just give me a deadline." Karla seemed like she was empowered by the planning, and Jade nodded her head.

"Speaking of deadlines and having something to do," Jade began, "Don't you think it's time to give me some responsibilities here?"

"Jade, enjoy your freedom," Karla told her, "because before you know it you will have a bunch of little ones running around and you will be fortunate not to have to worry about working." *There it was again. Karla wanted grandchildren.* Jade again thought of the text she had sent Sher. As soon as Karla would leave her office, Jade planned to check her cell phone again for any messages.

"So you plan to fire me then?" Jade asked, and Karla laughed.

"Of course not. That's what nannies are for if you want to work," Karla told her.

"Karla, I'm not working now. I'm asking you to make me feel productive, give me a little self worth. Even tending bar gave me that," Jade said, realizing she had left the comment slip.

"Don't even think about opening up a restaurant and bar. That would be too much work, too much time away from my son. You need to be at home at night. Keep track of when you ovulate, too. That's important for timely conception." Karla let those words roll off of her tongue as if she was giving Jade tips on a recipe.

"Thanks for the advice," Jade responded, feeling drained already. Her so-called work day had barely begun and she already was suffering from Karla Green overload.

"No need to be embarrassed, honey," Karla began again. "I was young and passionately in love once, too. I'm sure my son can't keep his hands off of you." Now that was just too much. Jade was disgusted knowing Karla was going *there* in her own mind. Brock was her son, for God's sake.

Jade wished she could use the excuse of having work to do, to chase Karla out, but she obviously didn't. "We're not trying to have a baby," Jade said, wondering why she was igniting this spark which could turn into a full-blown inferno with Karla.

"Oh, right," Karla said. "You really should be married first. And, as you said, the sooner the better!" Before Jade could respond, Karla's secretary buzzed the phone intercom on Jade's desk. "Mrs. Green, you're needed on line one."

Karla walked over to Jade's desk and picked up the phone. She spoke with a demanding, here I am, professional voice. After a few minutes, Jade was going to walk out of her office to grab a cup of coffee or something from the main lounge, but that's when she heard her cell phone beep. She had the volume on high from when she was running, and it obviously caught both her and Karla's attention. Jade watched Karla look down on the desk in front of her. Jade knew it was the sound of a text alert, and she was hoping it was not a response from her mother, with a picture of Aspen.

Jade stepped slowly toward her phone on the desk. Karla kept talking, but it was quite obvious she had looked directly at Jade's phone message. When Jade picked up the phone, she saw a picture of Aspen. She was sitting in the grass, wearing a purple seersucker one piece. Her blonde curls were getting longer. Her fuller face made her resemble Jade more. She was smiling big. Her eyes were bright and happy. Jade tried not to stare. She also tried not to give notice to the feeling of her heart swelling inside of her chest.

A moment later, Karla hung up the phone. "Who's the princess in the photo?" she immediately asked Jade.

"My cousin's child," Jade responded, believing she was safe with that answer as Karla had no idea Sadie's boys were only seventeen and nineteen years old.

"What a beauty. She looks like you, actually," Karla added, appearing quick to leave the room this time.

After she closed the office door behind her, Jade stared at her phone again. Aspen was beautiful. Jade could see that now. And then Jade saw the message her mother had texted and sent below the photo. *Your little girl is getting big.*

A pang of panic seared through Jade. *Had Karla read that? Most likely not, or she would have called her out on what it meant.*

In her own executive office, Karla was on the phone again. She needed the assistance of a business associate who owed her a favor. She wanted to run a background check, and possibly hire a private investigator, to send to O'Fallon, Illinois.

Chapter 23

"I received a text from Jade today. She asked me for a picture of Aspen. This is a good sign." Sher was in her work clothes, a white business suit with cropped pants and a short jacket. She wore a black sleeveless silk blouse under the jacket and chunky-heeled black sandals. She never knocked or rang the doorbell at Angie's house, she just opened the front door, walked through the living room and found her mother in the kitchen, sitting at the table eating dinner.

Angie put down a croissant, stuffed with chicken salad. She finished chewing the bite she had just taken, and then picked up her napkin to wipe her mouth and then her hands. "Did she say anything else?" Angie asked Sher as she pulled up a chair and sat down.

"She asked me not to ask her any questions, just please send a picture. I don't know mom, do we jump on this and not stop until she comes home? Or do we continue to give her space?" Sher was hopeful, but she knew Jade well and she was trying to remain focused on how this may not mean anything life-changing.

Angie was wearing white Bermuda shorts with a neon orange tank top. She had matching flip flops on her feet and her toes were painted pale pink. Sher admired her suntan as she spent her summer days inside of her school office. Her mother really knew how to take care of herself and it showed, but Sher would never tell her that. Compliments just weren't her style. It was never in the code of their relationship.

"I think we should push," Angie replied, speaking from personal experience. "Forty-five years ago, I graduated from college. I had been gone for four years. At that graduation ceremony, it hit me. Everyone was surrounded by family, everyone but me, because I abandoned mine. I was alone and it was my own goddamn fault. I started to feel regret, but I pushed those thoughts away and probably ended up drunk and having sex with a stranger I picked up at the bar on the Central West End." Sher looked away from her and down at her hands folded on top of the placemat on the table. It was still difficult to imagine her mother and all of the poor choices she made in her younger years. "Two days later, my mother showed up, with both you and Sadie in tow. That day changed my life."

Sher still remembered that day, vividly. "So you're saying if grandma had not forced your hand, you would not have come back to us?" Sher often wondered exactly that.

"That's a question I cannot answer. Dane's death changed things, too," Angie added. "What I'm saying is sometimes we're too proud, or too ashamed, and it's easier not to do anything."

"So, what are we waiting for? We need to take advantage of Jade's sudden inquiry about Aspen. I think you should take the lead, she listens to you, she loves you more." Angie didn't argue with her daughter because she knew it was true.

"When are you scheduled to have Aspen overnight again?" Angie asked Sher, knowing she sometimes kept her on weekends for Rhett.

"One week from tomorrow. Rhett is going to Vegas with a few of his friends and I agreed to keep Aspen from Friday to Sunday."

"Perfect. The three of us will be taking a road trip to Tennessee then." Angie already had a plan.

"To bring Jade her baby? We can't just drop her off? And shouldn't Rhett know if I'm taking his daughter five hours from home?" Sher felt panicked. She didn't operate like her mother. She was safer, and smarter, or so she liked to think.

"You make it sound as if we are kidnapping her. We're not. We are her family and it's time Jade visited with her baby. We will be bringing Aspen back home with us, and maybe Jade as well. This is our chance to water the seed that wants to grow in Jade's mind, and maybe even in her heart, too." Angie felt optimistic about this.

"Will you let Jade know you're coming to visit?" Sher asked.

"Of course, but she will believe I'm coming alone." Angie winked at her daughter.

"You'll never change," Sher said, trying not to love her mother. But, she did.

"You came to me for help and I intend to come through for you, and for Jadey." Angie patted Sher's hand on top of the table and Sher purposely squeezed it too tight.

***

Jade was excited about her grandmother coming to visit. She was concerned about her driving that long distance, alone, but Angie insisted she would be perfectly fine. Brock even offered to send a car for her, but she declined.

Angie's visit was three days away, and Jade had mentioned her excitement to Karla while at work. It was also Jade's way of hinting to Karla that she didn't want to be bothered with wedding plans, or even just her presence, throughout the weekend. When Karla said she wanted to meet Angie, Jade replied, *of course*, but never suggested she stop by the house while she's there. Jade was tolerating Karla as her wedding planner as she continued to put that front and center in all of their lives. Jade tried to remain focused on how happy Karla was about her son getting married.

"I dropped off two different bottles of wine at your house this morning," Karla told Jade in her office. "Both are red, and I want you to sample them. Your favorite will be the one served at the wedding reception with our meal." Jade preferred white wine, but she kept silent and gave in to Karla's desire.

"Sure, I will try both tonight," Jade answered her.

"Wonderful! Thank you," Karla said, leaving her office abruptly. It was unusual for her not to overstay until Jade was at her breaking point, but for whatever reason she was quick to leave today, and Jade was grateful.

***

Brock would be working late, through dinner, so when Jade made it home from work, she slipped off her dress clothes and left them on the floor in their bedroom as she found her favorite peach bikini, put it on, and went downstairs and outside to the pool. She wasn't hungry for dinner yet, she just wanted to soak up what was left of the sun for the day.

She stepped two steps into the pool and then submerged herself in the water up to her shoulders to get herself wet before getting back out of the pool to lay in the lounge chair.

Jade's eyes were closed behind her large, dark sunglasses and she nearly jumped out of her skin when she heard Karla's voice beside her. "May I disrupt you for a little wine tasting?" She was carrying two full glasses of red wine, Jade noticed, as she sat up straight in her chair and felt her heart beat quicken.

"Jesus, Karla, you startled me!" Jade was not thrilled to see her again. She sees her all day, every day, at work. Even the sight of seeing her walk by her office or through the glass in the conference room, made her cringe. Probably because she was the busy, important one in the office building. Jade didn't want to be important, she only wanted to be productive. And that had yet to happen.

"Oh, I'm so sorry, dear," Karla said, sounding sincere. "I just have no rest with this wine selection. I want your opinion. Here, these are both for you."

"Both?" Jade asked. "Aren't you having any with me?"

"No drinking before dinner for me, but thank you," Karla said. "Besides, I already know the one I would like to serve at the wedding." *Well then just serve that one,* Jade thought. *Everything else has been your preference, your idea, your everything.*

Instead of arguing, Jade took one of the glasses from her and took a sip of the wine. It was good, and Jade said so. She then reached for the other glass and Karla pulled back. "Oh no, finish it. Your taste buds may tire of the taste after more than one sip. I need you to be sure it's good until the last drop."

"You're going to get me drunk. I'm drinking on an empty stomach," Jade told her, and she laughed out loud. It was almost as if that was Karla's intention. Jade didn't care at the moment. Tolerating her drunk may be the way to go outside of the office.

Once Jade finished the first glass, she still said she enjoyed the taste. Karla switched the empty glass with the other full glass with her and Jade tried it, too.

"Ohhh... I like this one, better," Jade admitted.

"Well drink up to be sure again," Karla insisted.

When both glasses of wine were empty, Jade no longer cared what the two of them had been talking about. Yes, she would be able to make it to Karla's house for her first dress fitting on Saturday afternoon. Her grandmother would be in town, but she would plan on bringing her along. Sharing that experience with Angie would beat the hell out of sharing anything with Karla, Jade believed, feeling loopy as she thought she heard Karla say she was leaving. Then, Jade only closed her eyes for a moment after sitting back down on the lounge chair, poolside. When she opened them again, Karla was gone.

Her body felt sluggish as Jade tried to sit up to see if Karla was anywhere in sight out there. She found herself taking small, short breaths. She suddenly felt as though all the air was rushing out of her lungs and when she tried to inhale, it was difficult, almost as though she was breathing liquid. There was a sharp pain directly to the left of her sternum, and Jade placed her hand over it, applying pressure. She wanted to get up, go inside and maybe lay down on the couch or in bed. She was not feeling well at all. She blamed the wine. Too much on an empty stomach. Jade moved her legs off of the lounge chair and light-headedness immediately set in. She reached for her phone, beside her on the lounge chair. She didn't think she needed to call 911, but she knew she shouldn't be alone. The staff had all gone home for the day, so right now she was alone. The dizziness subsided for a moment as Jade kept her eyes focused on the text message she wanted to send to Brock. She knew he was in a meeting, but maybe he would see her message soon. She managed to type COME HOMW, missing the E and selecting the W instead. As she hit send, everything began to spin out of control. And, next, within seconds, Jade blacked out from the extreme pain. She felt as though her heart was being pulled to the center of her chest and as it was pounding like a drum.

Chapter 24

The meeting had just gotten started. It was a dinner meeting at Saffire among Brock, Clay, and two healthcare professionals. They were discussing building a new state-of-the-art physical therapy building in Franklin. Brock was giving the businessmen what he and his parents called the Green Construction spiel, how they provided clients with an unmatched level of reliability, expertise, proactive communication and cost effective solutions.

"Combined with our attention to detail this not only ensures that our projects are delivered on-time and within budget, but also that they result in superior quality," Brock told them, as he felt his cell phone vibrate in the back pocket of his jeans.

As Clay began to add his part, following his son, Brock reached for his phone to check his message. He had an eerie feeling. He knew he needed to see who was trying to contact him. He thought of Jade, because she was his life. And, because he still had flashbacks of the night he almost lost her. She was going to be his wife. It was his job to take care of her now.

When he read her message, he instantly found it strange. Jade never texted in all capital letters, and she had a pet peeve about misspellings. He laughed at her tendency to send corrections when the autocorrect flubbed a word or two in her texts. COME HOMW suddenly worried him. He could not concentrate on the meeting. "I have an emergency," he interrupted, standing up from the table, forcing the meeting to a halt. "Dad, you got this for me?" Clay shook his head yes, and told him to go. As his son rushed out of the restaurant, Clay apologized for him and continued on.

Brock drove too fast through the city and even faster to get to the outskirts to his estate. He left the door to his truck wide open after he pulled directly up to the house, slammed on the breaks and ran inside. He was more worried now because Jade had not answered his calls. He tried to reach her three times while driving home.

There was no answer when he called out her name as he ran through the main level of the house. He then raced up the stairway and into their bedroom. He found her clothes on a pile on the floor, but no Jade. He dashed to the large window in their bedroom and looked down at the pool, and saw her, lying still in the lounge chair. He begged God to let her just be sleeping as he raced to her, poolside.

He knew when he reached her that she was unconscious. He checked to see if she was still breathing, and she was, but it seemed shallow. He reached for his phone, again in the back pocket of his jeans, and felt panicked as he called 911.

It was like déjà vu for Brock, watching the paramedics do their job. And again, he begged God to *save her*. He watched them check her airway and then administer oxygen. One of the paramedics leaned close to her and appeared to be inhaling through his nose.

"Does your wife take any kind of prescription medication?" one of the male paramedics asked Brock. Brock said *no, nothing,* as he thought of her being called his wife. He wanted that so badly. *She just had to survive this. Whatever this was.*

Very little time passed and the two paramedics worked diligently together to load Jade onto a stretcher. "We think she overdosed," the same male paramedic said to Brock. We can smell alcohol on her breath. This appears to be a reaction to combining drugs and alcohol. We need to get her to the hospital now."

"Jade does not do drugs," Brock defended her.

"It could be something over-the-counter. Accidents like this happen frequently. The doctors will run some tests to figure this out. Just do them a favor and look around your house now." There was nothing in sight outside, not a single bottle or glass, if she had been drinking.

Brock rushed inside, and searched the kitchen within seconds. Nothing was found. He wasn't going to waste anymore time. He wanted to be on that ambulance's rear bumper on its way to the hospital.

Again, like the last time, Brock was waiting alone in the lounge near the hospital's emergency room. An hour had passed and he was growing increasingly worried, minute by minute. His assumed his father was still tied up in what was supposed to be their meeting. Otherwise, he would have called.

Brock stood up to pace the empty room and after about eight or ten times of back and forth, the doctor was standing in the doorway. "Mr. Green?" This doctor was bald with dark-rimmed square-rimmed glasses and appeared to be in his sixties.

"Yes," Brock nodded his head and felt impatient to hear the news about Jade. He just hoped with his entire being for the news to be good.

"Your wife combined a barbiturate with alcohol, and her body's reaction caused her to lose consciousness," the doctor told Brock.

"What the hell is a barbiturate?" Brock interjected.

"A sedative," he responded.

"That's crazy! Jade does not take sedatives." Brock knew her well now. She had no trouble falling asleep or staying asleep. In fact, he was a light sleeper and he liked to tease her about *sleeping like a rock* beside him.

"That is what the tests concluded," the doctor responded, calmly. He had been in the medical field for years, which was long enough to know that family, friends, and lovers did not always know everything there was to know. "We administered a cathartic with an activated charcoal to rid your wife's system of the toxins." Brock wanted to ask the doctor to give him the information in English, but he refrained when he understood his last statement. The poison was being removed from Jade's body. He didn't care how. *Just get rid of it. Get her well again.* "She is temporarily on a ventilator and comatose."

"Wait! What? Jade has a machine doing her breathing for her? And she's in a coma? What does that all mean? How bad is this really, doctor?" Brock felt panicked again. What he was hearing was not good. Not good at all.

"The treatment of barbiturate abuse or overdose is generally supportive," the doctor replied. "The amount of support required depends on the person's symptoms. If the patient is drowsy but awake and can swallow and breathe without difficulty, the treatment can be as simple as monitoring the patient closely. If the patient is not breathing, it may involve mechanical ventilation until the drug has worn off. That is the case with your wife. Her breathing was too shallow. The drug will wear off, our counteractive treatment will help speed up that process. I expect a full recovery," the doctor concluded.

Brock sighed, and he could have hugged the medicine man in front of him right now. Jade would recover. That was all he needed to know.

It was difficult for him to see Jade hooked up to a breathing machine, and even more trying for him to sit beside her, hold her hand, touch her face, talk to her, and receive no response. Jade never moved or opened her eyes. Nurses were in and out of her room, constantly monitoring Jade's condition. *She's improving*, they assured him, and finally after two hours, Brock stepped out into the hallway to call his parents.

He reached Clay first, still feeling surprised he had not followed up with him about the emergency which forced him to leave their meeting early. Brock told his father what the doctor believed had happened and Clay's reaction was shock and immediate worry. "Dear God, son! Is she going to be okay?"

"She looks awful, but yes they tell me she will make a full recovery," Brock answered. "But, dad, it's scary as hell to see her hooked up to a ventilator and unresponsive."

Clay was still worried and he told Brock his mother was not home, but as soon as she arrived they would be at the hospital to support him, and Jade.

***

The night turned into morning and Brock remained in the chair beside Jade's bed. He never slept. He just kept watching her, and sought reassurance from every nurse who came into that hospital room all night long.

His parents never showed at the hospital, and Brock again felt surprised. With anything else, his mother never missed a chance to be there, to be involved.

It was midday before Brock got ahold of his mother. This time he called her instead of his father. "Mom, where are you? I thought you and dad were coming up to the hospital?"

"I assumed the hospital had a strict visiting hour's policy throughout the night," Karla replied. "We've called to check on her condition, honey. She's going to be alright, isn't she?"

"That's what they keep telling me," Brock told her. "I just don't understand what happened. I need her to wake up so she can explain this."

"I'm sure it was not intentional," Karla replied. "Medication and alcohol can really screw things up sometimes. The reaction just depends on the person."

"That's what the doctor said," Brock stated. "I just know Jade does not take medication. I have never even seen her pop an ibuprofen for a headache."

After Brock ended his conversation with his mother, one that he felt she cut short on her end, he walked back into Jade's room where a nurse he had not seen yet was present.

"Say hello to sleeping beauty," the nurse told him, as he quickly glanced from her, to the bed, to Jade. She had her eyes open. He rushed to her side, kneeling down on the floor because it was quicker than sitting down in a chair and sliding it closer to her.

"You okay?" he asked, softly. She was looking at him. She was responsive. And, he noticed the ventilator had already been removed.

"I think so," she responded with a raspy sound in her voice.

"What happened?" he asked, hoping she could explain.

"I don't remember, my mind is just so fuzzy right now," she told him. "What did the doctor say?"

"He said your body had a serious reaction to mixing drugs and alcohol," Brock stated, as the nurse stepped out of the room. She had already paged the doctor to examine Jade.

"I don't take drugs," she said, instantly. "I did have some wine. I remember, two glasses." Jade thought of Karla saying she had dropped off two kinds of red wine for her to sample for the wedding reception, to be served with dinner. Then, she recalled Karla bringing it to her, poolside. And telling her to drink all of both. "Brock, what kind of drug was found in my system?"

"A sedative," he answered.

Shockwaves seared through Jade's body, and chill bumps formed on her arms. Her hands were trembling, and Brock was watching her very closely. He could tell she was remembering something. But, he had absolutely no idea what she was thinking right now.

Jade flashbacked in her memory to her conversation with Pamela in the park. *She can't sleep at night. She suffers from insomnia. She's dependant on her prescription medicine.*

"Jade? Talk to me? Are you remembering something?" Brock sat closer and tried to be patient as he awaited her response.

Oh my God... Your mother poisoned me! Your mother tried to kill me! Jade's thoughts were racing. She had to be absolutely certain before she accused Karla Green of attempted murder.

Chapter 25

Jade never told Brock what she had pieced together. *Karla was to blame.* Jade started to get tired while they were talking and she told Brock she felt like she needed to rest. He stayed with her while she dozed in and out of sleep, and finally she suggested he go home to shower and get some rest, too.

"I would rather stay here with you, to make sure you're okay," Brock said to her, still with so much worry in his eyes.

"You're too good to me, Green," she said, smiling at him.

"Get used to it," he replied, taking her hand in his. "Just, please, stop scaring the shit of out of me with regular emergency room visits. I can't take anymore. I can't lose you."

Jade lifted his hand up to her mouth and kissed his fingers. "I'm not going anywhere, I promise."

***

She was supposed to be sleeping, but she couldn't rest her mind. As Jade laid there, in that hospital bed, and replayed what she remembered happening, she was certain Karla had poisoned her.

Next to her bedside was Brock's cell phone. He purposely left it there for her as she did not have one with her. Jade's cell phone was back at the house and Brock told her he would bring it to her when he returned in a few hours. In the meantime, he suggested she keep his phone in case she needed to contact him.

Jade took Brock's cell phone in her hands as she came up with an idea. She found Karla's contact information and sent her a text, pretending to be Brock. *Mom, come to the hospital as soon as you can. I need you.*

Jade was sure that would work. Karla would come rushing to Brock's side, expecting to comfort him because Jade was either dying or had already died. That, afterall, was what she wanted. It was her intention when she tried to poison her. Jade was certain of it.

It took about thirty seconds for Karla to reply to the text she thought came from her son. *On my way,* was all she said, and Jade laid her head back on the pillow in her hospital bed and closed her eyes. She needed to save her strength. She was going to need it to deal with Karla.

Jade could hear her out at the nurse's station, requesting the room number of her son's fiancé. Jade knew Karla was expecting to find Brock in her room, so she remained still in bed as Karla made her way in there.

Her eyes looked closed, but she had them open just enough to see Karla had walked in, wearing a red business suit with a very short skirt. Jade watched her search around the room, turning her head side to side. When she realized Brock was not in there, she stared from afar at Jade. Jade could feel her heart pounding inside of her chest. This woman was incredibly dangerous.

Karla began to walk toward her, and when she got close enough to her bedside, Jade purposely popped her eyes wide open. "Oh dear God!" Karla gasped, bringing her hand to her chest. "You frightened me!" She took two steps backward. "You're okay? You're no longer on a ventilator or in a coma. Well, that's wonderful." Jade allowed her to speak, and then she responded.

"Disappointed?" Jade asked her, as she lifted her head up and sat upright in bed. Her full strength was returning.

"No, of course not. Relieved is more like it," Karla tried to sound convincing.

"I'm glad you're here," Jade told her.

"You are? Well, thank you. I thought I would find Brock, but better yet I'm seeing you awake and recovering." Karla smiled, and Jade wanted to wipe that smile off of her face with a hard smack of her bare hand across it.

"I'm glad you're here," Jade repeated, "because I need your help. My memory is fuzzy still, but bits and pieces are slowly coming together. I know what happened to me."

"Oh?" Karla asked, refraining from saying more.

"I recall our wine tasting by the pool, or rather, my wine tasting as you insisted I drink both full glasses."

Karla showed no emotion to give away whether she was nervous or disappointed in Jade remembering she was there, with wine. "Honey, I had no idea you had medication in your system." That was all Karla replied as if it was Jade's fault for being irresponsible. Or stupid.

"I do not take medication and I never took any last night," Jade said, holding her own.

"The tests showed otherwise," Karla said, almost with a sneer.

"The tests showed a prescription sedative in my system," Jade began, "and I'll have you know I sleep well without any assistance. Funny though, that's not what I've heard about you. I was at the park recently, sitting on a bench after a run, and I had a very interesting conversation with a woman you used to know. Pamela was her name, and you seem to have left a very sour taste in her mouth. She happened to mention how you have trouble sleeping." Karla tried to hide the surprise in her eyes. The kind of surprise that instantly showed.

"That woman is history. She used my son. What does she care if I sleep well at night?" Karla was trying to find a way out of this. But, she knew Jade knew.

"I don't think she cares at all. She was just making conversation." Jade was feeling the power of having the upper hand right now.

"I have a meeting to get to at the office," Karla said,

looking at her diamond watch and beginning to back away.

"Not until you help me figure out why in the world my fiancé's mother would want me dead." Jade remained calm, and her words were barely a whisper, but Karla had heard every single one.

She stepped closer to Jade's bedside. "There's no place for you in my son's life. You're trash. Go back to being a bartender at a rundown tavern. Reunite with your first husband. I've heard how you broke his heart."

Jade now knew Karla did some investigating. That was the way Karla operated. With money. With power. "Don't forget to mention my baby," Jade said, without flinching. "You did see my phone that day. Her photo and the text message. Go on, call me on it."

"I wanted you to be the one for my son, but there was something off from the moment I met you," Karla glared at her while she spoke. "Without my son's money, you are nothing."

"No, without your son's love, I felt worthless. He has brought more meaning to my life than I could have ever imagined." Jade was being honest. "Knowing who I was before, or what I went through in my life has not changed Brock's feelings for me. He loves me, and there's not a damn thing you can do about it. Well, you tried, but you failed. I'm still breathing."

"That's absurd and no one will believe trash over me." Karla turned on her heels and walked all the way to the door before she stopped when Jade spoke again.

"Do you hear that?" Jade asked her.

Karla stood silently and attempted to listen in disgust. "Hear what?" She turned, and started to push open the door.

"The ticking. It's like a time bomb. Enjoy your freedom while it lasts. Oh, and try to sleep well."

Karla rushed out of the door without looking back, and Jade sat against her propped up pillow in bed. She wore a smile on her face, and she was quick to reach for Brock's cell phone again, by her bedside. She put her finger on the touch screen. Exactly eight minutes and twenty-two seconds had gone by, and were recorded on the phone.

Chapter 26

"We need to talk," was the first thing Jade said to Brock when he returned to her bedside at the hospital.

"Okay," he said, sitting down in the chair beside her bed and placing her cell phone next to his on the table.

"My memory is not fuzzy. I know what happened to me last night," Jade began. "I came home from work, put on my swimsuit, and went out to the pool. I was not out there very long and your mother showed up. She told me she had two different kinds of red wine for me to sample and choose between for the wedding reception. She insisted I drink both glasses, and she left after both were gone."

"I don't understand," Brock interrupted. "That doesn't explain why your tests showed drugs in your system. Do you remember taking anything before drinking with my mother?" And now Brock was also wondering why Karla had not told him she was at the house with Jade.

"Your mother was not drinking. Only me," Jade told him. "Brock, this is going to seem like a strange question, but are you aware of your mother having trouble sleeping?"

Brock paused before answering her. Jade watched his eyes widen. "She has taken sleeping pills for years, why?"

"The sedative the doctor found in my system was in the wine. That's the only explanation." Jade didn't hold back. She accused his mother. She would swear on her life she almost lost that this was the truth.

"You think my mother drugged you?" Brock scoffed, and shook his head. "That's ridiculous!"

"She found out about my past, she must have had a background check done. She knows everything, even about Aspen. I'm not good enough for you, in her eyes. She wanted me gone in the worst way." Jade's voice remained calm, but she was nervous and scared to be telling him all of this.

"My mother is not a murderer. You're accusing her of attempted murder, Jade. You're obviously not thinking clearly." Brock was worried about her. This would destroy her relationship with his mother if Karla found out what Jade was accusing her of.

"Listen to me, Brock. I confronted her. We argued. She is

guilty. I don't know where we go from here, but I am not safe around her. She is dangerous."

Brock leaned forward and put his face in his hands. When he looked up at her, he looked forlorn. "Are you okay, Jade? This does not make any sense. You're talking crazy."

Crazy was what happened next. The door to Jade's hospital room opened and in walked Angie. Brock never had a chance to tell Jade how he called her grandmother last night. He had to. She was Jade's family. And, now, he was glad he had contacted her. If anyone could talk some sense into Jade, it was this woman. Jade, on the other hand, was thinking exactly the opposite. *Her Gram would be on her side.*

"Jadey..." Angie spoke first. "What in the world happened?" That was the burning question. Jade had the answer now. But, so far, Brock did not believe her.

"Hug me first, Gram," Jade said, as Brock stepped back for Angie to move in closer to the bed, and to Jade. Being in her arms felt like home. Jade missed the normalcy that Angie brought to her life, and she had not clearly realized that until now.

Brock spoke as the two of them parted from each other's arms. "I will let you two visit. I'm going to see my mother." Jade just looked at him. She didn't know what to say, so she said nothing. She just hoped he would believe her, and not Karla.

When Brock left, Angie sat down in the chair he had been sitting on beside the bed. She was wearing dark washed denim capris, a white cotton short-sleeved shirt with a scoop neckline and a ruffled trim, and white and gray boat shoes with no-show white socks. Jade thought she looked as beautiful as ever.

"I sense some tension between the two of you," Angie said, directly. "Want to talk about it?"

"Well, Gram, I almost died and his mother was the one who tried to kill me!"

"Excuse me? " Angie asked, moving to the edge of her seat.

And that's when Jade explained the entire story. When she got to the part about recording her conversation with Karla, she reached for Brock's cell phone on the table beside her bed, but it was gone. Only hers was sitting there. She had never seen Brock pick it up, but he must have and taken it with him.

"You have to press charges!" Angie demanded.

"I have to convince Brock first," Jade replied, and Angie was instantly worried Jade may have rushed into changing her life only to end up broken again. But, at least she was alive. And now Angie was going to make it her mission to bring Jade back home, safe, with her. For good.

***

Twice, while they were talking, Jade and Angie were interrupted. First, the doctor came into the room and told Jade she would be under observation at the hospital for one more night and then tomorrow morning she could go home. Jade was happy to know she would be released, but that moment of feeling like everything was going to be okay was short-lived when the door opened up again and Sher was standing there.

Leave it to her mother to complicate her life. She was holding Aspen in her arms.

Jade wanted to be angry. Was this some kind of a joke, or game her mother and grandmother were playing? To show up with her baby, right here, right now, when she was most vulnerable, was not fair.

"What are you doing?" Jade asked Sher, and then looked unhappily at Angie too.

"There are four generations in this room right now," Angie spoke as Sher remained standing from afar. Aspen was looking at Jade with curiosity in her eyes, but she clung to Sher for reassurance. "We're here to make you see where you belong, united with your family."

Jade looked closely at Aspen. She was not a baby anymore. She was getting big, growing, and looking more like a little girl. Jade could see herself in her, just as she could in the picture Sher had sent her. That was the picture Karla had seen. The message in that text was what set Karla off. She wanted her out of Brock's life, and at this moment Jade did not know what she wanted. It was blatantly obvious that her mother and grandmother had joined forces to change her mind.

Aspen wiggled her way out of Sher's arms and began walking around the room. At thirteen months, she was steady on her feet and curious about everything around her. "Is she doing okay?" Jade asked her mother.

"Yes, Rhett takes very good care of her. She's healthy and growing and such a joy..." Sher's words trailed off. Jade watched her again. She wondered who bought her the little yellow dress she was wearing, and those little white sandals. A mother should know those kinds of things. But, Jade had not been much of a mother since Aspen was born. She told herself she was right all along, *Aspen was much better off without her.*

Aspen kept Sher on her feet, following after her to make sure she did not hurt herself or touch anything she shouldn't. It took her about ten minutes of roaming around before she made her way closer to Jade. She was babbling, but Jade could not make out her words. Not until she placed her little hands on the bed's mattress and tried to lift her body up onto the bed next to Jade. "Up," she said, clearly, and Jade looked at Sher, behind her.

"She wants to sit by you," Sher said, and Jade could feel both her and Angie's eyes on her. She glanced at them both. They shared looks of wonderment. *What in the world will Jade do now? This little girl needs her.* Jade reached out her arms and placed her hands around Aspen's torso. She felt strong enough to lift her, and so she did. Aspen seemed content. It was as if she knew her mother's touch.

Jade set her down on the bed sheet beside her, and she watched Aspen pull the blanket up and over her head. Jade heard a muffled giggle and she smiled at both Angie and Sher. The looks on their faces were one in the same. It was as if they wanted to say, *See, we told you...she is a joy...her personality lights up a room...you can't help but love her.*

When Aspen popped her head out from underneath the covers, she found Jade's hand on her lap. She touched her finger that the immense diamond ring was on. After a brief fascination with the sparkly stone, Jade felt Aspen's whole hand wrapped around her thumb and pointer finger. There was a surge of something happening inside of Jade. She did not have chill bumps on her arms, she did not have a smile on her face, or even a light in her eyes. Nothing showed on the outside. But, every positive feeling imaginable came alive in the inside of her mind, heart, and soul. This was the way it was supposed to be. This child, her child, was a part of her.

Sher was studying her daughter's face and had absolutely no idea what she was thinking, feeling, wanting to happen now and for the rest of her life. Was it a mistake for them to bring Aspen to her? Were her feelings still cold? Angie, also watching Jade closely, knew. She had been there. It was happening. Jade felt as she had after time had gone by, and she finally realized where she was meant to be. Angie dabbed her eyes with a tissue she had in her front jean's pocket. They may have been three hundred miles away, but Angie was sure Jadey, beside her little girl right now, was home.

***

Aspen was ready to let go of Jade's fingers before Jade was ready for her to let go. She wanted down, to explore the room some more, and Sher followed her again. They talked very little about what had happened to force Jade to be hospitalized, but Sher did tell her she was happy to know she was being released tomorrow. Angie told Jade that the three of them were staying at a hotel in Nashville and Jade immediately invited them to stay with her and Brock at the house. "We will work out those details tomorrow, once you're out of this hospital," Angie told her. Jade wanted them to stay a few days, but she was not sure what was happening between her and Brock. She needed to talk to him again and find out what his mother told him. She also needed to be sure Angie kept quiet, so when Jade pulled her close for a hug, she whispered into her ear for her not to say anything about Brock's mother. For now.

As Aspen waved goodbye to Jade, she felt something again. *Goodbye*, she said, waving back to her, thinking, *but, I hope not for long.*

While Jade waited for Brock to return she sat upright in her hospital bed, with her knees pulled up to her chest, thinking. The ring on her finger was her future. It symbolized a whole new world for her. She loved Brock and desperately wanted to be with him, but everything else had come to mean nothing. She didn't need the estate and all its extravagance. And, she certainly didn't need Karla. But, Brock did need all of it. Including his mother.

Jade had to make a choice now. And the strange part about the timing of seeing Aspen again was she knew what she had to do. As a mother, she could now grasp Karla's love for Brock. She didn't condone how crazy she was, but she did understand Karla wanting the best of everything for her son. Brock was a part of Karla, just as Aspen was a part of her. Jade wanted all good things for her little girl. She always had. It was just different now, because she wanted to share every bit of it with her.

Chapter 27

They were both quiet when Brock returned. Jade waited for him to speak and he didn't quite know what to say to her. He was worried about her, and his mother had fed him with lies to enhance his worry.

"Your silence is making me nervous," Jade told him as he sat down again in the chair beside her bed. She was tired of being in that bed and she wanted to go home with him.

"Are you feeling any better?" Brock spoke.

"Yes, and I am ready to get out of here," Jade answered. "The doctor came in and he said he's releasing me tomorrow."

"I know," Brock smiled and nodded his head. "I spoke to him in the hallway, on my way in." Brock had, in fact, spoken with him in detail about Jade's condition. The doctor assured him if her memory was unclear, it would return to normal before too long. "I have a surprise for you," he added, and she just looked at him. "You're going home tonight. As long as you're not alone, and you won't be because I'm not leaving your side, the doctor will sign off on your release tonight."

"Thank you, there's no one else I'd rather be with tonight," she said, wondering how many more nights she had left with this man who mirrored a knight in shining armor in her eyes.

"Not even your Gram?" Brock asked. "Where is she by the way? Will she be staying with us for awhile?"

"She's at a hotel in Nashville, until tomorrow, because she thought I had another night to spend here," Jade answered.

"Well I can go get her, or send a car," Brock offered. "I don't like the idea of her being alone."

"She's not alone," Jade answered. "She brought my mother with her...and Aspen." Jade held her breath. How was she going to explain to Brock what was happening inside of her heart when she couldn't even explain it to herself?

"Your baby?" Brock asked, surprised. "Was she here? Did you see her?" Jade nodded her head. "How did that go?"

"It was nice to see her," Jade began. "I can't believe how much she has grown. She's not a baby anymore. She's the sweetest, cutest little girl I've ever seen."

Brock smiled at her. "Of course she is, she's yours."

"Mine," Jade replied. "Something's changed for me, Brock, and I don't know how to explain it because I can't even comprehend it."

"Are you ready to be a part of her life?" Brock asked. It was the way he asked if she was *ready* that made Jade love him even more. He understood her. He knew, for a very long time, she was not ready to be a mother. But, yes, now she felt like she was.

"I think so," Jade replied.

"You know that does not change anything between us," Brock stated, sincerely. "I will love her because you do."

Jade reached for his hand and held it on the side of the bed. "I don't deserve you." And, after she said those words, she wished she hadn't. That was probably what his mother had just drilled into his mind.

"Not true," Brock said, lifting up her hand to his mouth and kissing her fingers. "I love you."

"I love you, too. Let's go home."

***

Once they arrived at the estate, Brock thought he had to help Jade inside. He attempted to hold her up while she walked, and she laughed. "I'm okay, really. I feel strong as the doctor said I would once my system was clean again. So, don't try to tuck me into bed right away. I am sick of being in bed."

"What if I crawled in there with you?" he asked.

"Well, now that would be one way to entice me to lay down," she responded, giggling, and the two of them ended up sitting close on the couch after they walked into the house, entering the massive living room with twenty-two foot ceilings.

"Can I get you something to eat, or drink?" Brock asked her, as she slipped off her sandals and curled her legs up underneath her. She was wearing a pair of black yoga pants and a white tank top. Brock, always in jeans and boots, was wearing a red t-shirt.

"I just want to talk," she said, seriously. "I want to hear what happened when you confronted your mother."

"I didn't confront her, Jade," he said, trying to choose his words carefully, but being honest as he always was with her. "You've been through such an ordeal. You could not have been thinking clearly when you accused her of trying to kill you."

Jade tried to remain calm, because she did not want to overexert herself. "What did the two of you talk about then?"

"Getting you better. Being patient with you while you recover. My mother understands. She's not angry with you. She is willing to put this craziness behind you both and move on. She brought up our wedding plans again." Jade could not believe Brock's words. *Of course, Karla wanted to put the craziness behind her. She was the one behind it!*

"I know how much you love her," Jade spoke, calmly. "I've tolerated things from her because I respect your relationship with her, I wanted her to like me, and I tried to keep the peace. I can't do that anymore. Drugging me, walking away while I began to suffer, and wanting me to die is just beyond crazy." Jade wanted to add, *she is crazy,* but she had said enough already.

"I think we all just need to give it time," Brock said, remembering how his mother had said that to him, and he was cautious not to say Jade was wrong. He didn't believe his mother was capable of attempting murder, but Jade was entirely too fragile to hear those words from him now.

"I'm sure your mother suggested that as well," Jade said, boldly. "But, I'm not going to hide how I feel. I know the truth."

"So what does that mean?" Brock asked her, worried about her mindset, and also fearing what could happen to his mother's reputation if Jade's accusation would go public.

"Do you have your cell phone in your pocket?" Jade asked him, and he reached for it and put it in her hand, refraining from asking questions. Jade touched the screen and retrieved the audio she had recorded of her and Karla in the hospital. Jade began to play it, and maximized the volume so Brock would not miss a single word.

It was all there. The entire eight minutes and twenty-two seconds of Jade and Karla swapping words, harsh words, and by the time the recording ended, Brock was in disbelief.

There was no mistake. He heard his mother's voice saying, *There's no place for you in my son's life. You're trash. Go back to being a bartender at a rundown tavern. I wanted you to be the one for my son, but there was something off from the moment I met you. Without my son's money, you are nothing.*

And finally, Brock heard his mother say to Jade, *No one will believe trash over me.*

The audio ended and Jade sat back on the couch and waited for Brock to respond to what he had just heard. The truth was sometimes a hard pill to swallow.

"I wish you had told me that you saw Pamela, and I wish you had shared with me that you received a text about Aspen and somehow my mother intercepted it," Brock said, with obvious pain in his eyes.

"As I said," Jade responded. "I've kept quiet so many times just to keep the peace. I'm done living like that. For chrissakes, it almost cost me my life!"

"I know," Brock said, "and I'm so sorry. I heard her. She didn't deny it. Jade, does this mean..." he paused before he continued. "Does this mean you're going to press charges against my mother?" Brock knew having the audio and minimal investigating at the pharmacy, if Karla had used her own prescription medication, would be solid evidence to send his mother to prison. He was scared for her, but ashamed as well. He almost lost his fiancé because of his mother.

"No," Jade answered, instantly. "I am not going to bring this to the police. I won't lie to you though, I wanted to. I wanted her to pay. But, not anymore. Things changed. Now, I just want out."

"Out?" Brock panicked.

"How can I be your wife now? I will always be looking over my shoulder because your mother wanted to off me. I don't want the joke of a job she gave me, I don't want to share you with her. I want her out of my life, but I cannot ask you to want her out of yours. I know what she means to you." Jade was fighting the urge to cry. She had to be strong. This was the right thing to do. Her choice suddenly felt incredibly impromptu, but she knew she had to go forward with it.

"That's not fair," he said to her. "You cannot make this decision for us. This is our life, dammit! Don't run away from what we have!"

"Brock," Jade said, moving her face closer to his as they sat on the couch. "I can't ask you to give up everything for me. It's not realistic. Your home, your whole life, is right here. Mine is not. I'm going back to O'Fallon. I have a child who needs me."

"No, please," Brock begged her. "We can work this out. Just stay and figure this out with me. I'll hire the best lawyer for you. Maybe you and Rhett can work out some sort of shared custody. I could fly Aspen back and forth, if needed. You can get her back, have her in your life, and not have to walk away from our plans, our dreams, our life."

"This, all of this, is *your* life, Brock. You brought me to it, squeezed me into it, but I never quite fit right. I guess I'm a little rough around the edges," she tried to smile, or even make him laugh, but neither one of them felt like being remotely happy about what was happening. This was incredibly sad. This was the end of a great love story. It could have been great, anyway, had it been meant to be.

"What can I do to change your heart?" Brock asked her, and she wore a look of sheer surprise on her face.

"Why did you say it like that?" she asked, remembering when her Gram told her she could come home anytime, if she were to have a change of heart.

"Because I had your heart from the moment we met. I could see it, feel it. You were supposed to be Jade Green, remember? You still can be."

"The confidence you carry, and your confidence in me, has changed me. I am a better, stronger, person because of you." Jade was crying now. She knew this was goodbye. Brock may not have been ready to accept it, but he would in time.

Brock pulled her close and held her. She could hear his heart beating through his chest, pounding in her ear. She stayed in his arms for the longest time, until he made the first move to carry her upstairs, lay her down on the bed, and then he made love to her for the last time.

Chapter 28

Neither one of them slept. They just held onto to each other all night long. By not closing their eyes and drifting off to sleep, they were able to savor every second of the time they had left together.

At sunrise, Jade knew she had to call her grandmother. She needed the address to their hotel in Nashville. She intended to pack her bags and take a taxi to them. As if Brock had been reading her mind, he asked her what she was planning. "How much more time do I have left with you?"

"I will be leaving with my family today," she told him, and he insisted she drive her Jeep. It was his gift to her. "I can't," she resisted, "and you need to take this, too," she said, removing her engagement ring.

"I won't take it back," he fought. "It was meant to be yours."

Jade placed it on her pillow and got out of the bed. Brock never spoke, moved, or followed after her. He only laid back on his own pillow, stared up at the ceiling, and allowed the tears to trickle from his eyes and roll off his face.

She took a shower, got dressed, and packed four suitcases. She decided to take the clothes, all of it, which she had bought with Brock's money. There was no use in leaving it behind. He wanted her to have it, and she knew it would be a very long time before she would be able to afford anything nice for herself. She needed to get a job and be able to support herself, and now Aspen. It seemed like a long road, but Jade knew she would have her grandmother and her mother by her side. She would not be too proud anymore to ask for their help until she got back on her feet, and made a good life for herself and for her daughter.

Brock helped her carry all of her suitcases downstairs. She had asked him to call a taxi and he responded, *already taken care of.*

When Jade walked outside to meet her ride, she found Brock loading her suitcases into the back of the red Jeep he had given her. "Wait, no, Brock. I can't. I won't."

"You can," he responded. "I don't need it. You do. Think of Aspen," he reminded her. Don't be too proud to take it. Let me do this one last thing for you." As he said those words, he thought of himself as a coward. It was his own fault that he felt like his heart was being ripped out from his chest. He was the one allowing her to go, allowing them to end. It didn't have to be that way. He freely chose his mother, his position in the family business, his estate, the only life he knew. Over Jade. He chose it all over love. And he did love her with all of his heart.

The scene defined absolute heartbreak as they held on to each other one last time, and shared one final, tender kiss before they parted and Jade drove away in the red Jeep Brock had gifted to her.

Jade left her Jeep parked outside of the hotel, completely packed. She had not planned to stay in Tennessee one more day, or night. It was just too painful knowing Brock was still close by. And too tempting to run back to him.

She knocked once on the door of room one-twenty-one, and Angie answered. Both she and Sher were waiting and wondering why Jade wanted to come to them today. They had expected to join her and Brock at the estate for a couple days. They had no idea Jade was released from the hospital last night and driving a packed Jeep to go back home with the three of them.

"Jadey," Angie said, pulling her into a hug as she looked over her Gram's shoulder and saw Aspen asleep on one of the queen-sized beds and Sher seated in an armchair near the patio door.

"She's still asleep?" Jade asked, knowing it was ten o'clock in the morning and recognizing how she was not wearing pajamas but another cute little lime green dress with a white ruffled diaper cover.

"She was awake a lot last night as she had a little trouble sleeping in a strange place, strange bed," Sher explained as she got up from the chair and walked over to her mother and her daughter. "So, spill it, what is going on?" Sher asked Jade.

"I need a minute," Jade said to both of them as she walked over and sat on the bed beside her sleeping child. Jade moved her hand through the loose blonde curls, messy on her head. She leaned down and moved her lips to Aspen's forehead, then on the tip of her nose, and finally on her sweet lips. Her skin was so soft and the scent on her skin was intoxicating. Jade was there. She was in the place she begged to be for so long. This baby, this little girl, this child of hers, was absolutely amazing. Why had she not seen that before would forever remain a mystery. But, now, mattered more than the past she no longer could change.

Angie and Sher watched Jade in silence, and both were thinking opposite thoughts. Sher, always the pessimist with very little faith in her daughter, believed this was Jade's way of telling Aspen goodbye. She had come to them, at their hotel, to keep them away from her new life. And now she would ask them to go back home, and never return with Aspen again. Angie had an altogether different view of how it was finally happening. It was as if Jade was seeing her baby for the first time. Angie had been there, it had happened to her, too, and still she could not explain it. The tender touches, the kisses as she inhaled. All of it meant something now. Angie was certain

Jade had a change of heart.

Aspen remained asleep as Jade left her side and asked both Angie and Sher to hear her out. The three of them stood in the middle of the two beds, close to Aspen.

"A lot has happened in the time I've been away," Jade began. She and Brock had been together for nearly eight months from the time she met him at Shooters until now. "I made the conscious decision to change my life, and now I'm making another one to be a mother to my baby again. I'm moving back home." Angie was thinking, *that's my girl*, and Sher was thinking, *it's about goddamn time!*

"I don't know what to say," Sher spoke first. "Are you sure? Be sure because your baby girl knows what the hell is going on now. She's smart and she's perceptive and it doesn't take much love and attention for her to adapt to someone and expect them to be in her life." Sher was speaking from experience. She had planted herself in Aspen's life and quickly reaped the benefits of being on the receiving end of that precious little girl's love. She did not want to see her heart-broken if Jade were to run again.

"Don't you dare put that kind of fear in her!" Angie interrupted, trying to keep her voice low. "It has taken Jadey a very long time to get to this point. Allow her to relish in it." Sher rolled her eyes at her mother, and Jade thought how some things never change. There was love present in their dysfunctional family, but there was a sure supply of bickering, too.

"I'm sure," Jade said. And then she told them both the entire story, including the Karla saga. She didn't get teary-eyed when she spoke of leaving Brock, but she did feel like her heart was in her throat. For all she knew, that feeling may stay with her for the rest of her life. She would never want to share her heart, or her life, with another man. Brock was it for her. But, he was gone. She could now foresee herself leading the same type of life as Angie had. Finally focused on being a mother, and otherwise alone.

Both Angie and Sher were in Jade's corner. They despised Karla Green for going past the point of crazy and harming Jade, and they admired Brock for what he brought into Jade's life, and for knowing when to let her go.

Jade was behind the wheel of her red Jeep on Interstate 24 West. The windows were up and the top was closed. She was following Angie, driving her white Lincoln MKZ with Sher beside her in the passenger seat. They didn't have Aspen with them, in the backseat. This time, she was with her mommy. Jade looked up and into her rearview mirror and saw her, sitting in her car seat, looking from side to side and out of both windows. She was content, and Jade was feeling both excited and nervous to finally be focused on sharing a lifetime with her daughter.

***

When Rhett walked into Sher's house to pick up Aspen, his heart was about to pound through his chest. He had seen the red Jeep parked on the driveway. He wondered if this day would come. He certainly had no inkling of when it would happen, how soon, or if ever. But, despite how nervous he felt not knowing what to expect from her this time, he was prepared.

Since leaving Nashville, Jade had spent a solid twenty-four hours with Aspen. She jumped in with both feet. She wanted to play with her and take care of her. She helped her eat, bathed her, and watched her sleep. Jade had won Aspen over, she received her with a warm welcome. She was still too little to realize her mother had been distant for the first ten months of her life, and then absent for a few months, but was now back in her life. Jade was going to live with Sher, indefinitely. She was the one who helped Rhett care for Aspen the most. None of them were sure if Rhett would put up a fight, maybe even take Jade to court in order to settle a custody arrangement. Jade knew a lot of pieces had to fall into place. She had to get a job, for starters. Shared custody was Jade's goal, and she hoped Rhett would be compliant.

"Well, hello, Jade," Rhett said, as soon as he entered the living room of Sher's five-bedroom, two-story, white brick house on Ravenwood Circle. Jade was seated with Aspen on the light oakwood floor in front of the black leather sectional, playing with a pile of toys, and she was dressing a baby doll for her.

"Hi, Rhett. How was Vegas?"

"Too much fun," he replied. She sized him up in his white tennis shoes, baggy jeans and oversized heather gray t-shirt which was tucked in and bloused over his black belt entirely too much. He was thin and his clothes didn't fit. "How was Tennessee?" He held his breath, wondering if her time away was *just a trip*.

"Memorable," she answered, "but now I'm back, where I belong, with my daughter."

"What changed?" Rhett asked, trying not to reveal his disappointment. He had learned to live without her. She was depressing and she was not a good mother to their child. Then, she broke his heart when she chose another man over him.

"I have no words to explain it," she admitted, "but I'm Aspen's mother and I have every right to be as much a part of her life as you. I'm confident we can work something out. I will be living here for awhile to make things easier." Rhett wanted to say, *easier because you have no job and no lover boy or his money to spend?*

"When you walked out," Rhett began, "I had some good people in my life to help me pick up the pieces, or rather to hold those pieces together. My parents, your mother, and your grandmother have all been there, and they've been wonderful. And then I started thinking about the future. I wanted to secure what's mine. A lawyer helped me to do that. I can email you the official documents tonight after I get back to the house with Aspen."

"What documents?" Jade interrupted, careful not to get angry, but she was close. *What had he done?*

"I was granted sole legal custody of my daughter," he revealed. "When there is only one parent in the picture, for example, if one parent has abandoned the child or disappeared, the court after carefully considering all of the facts and evidence, will determine what's in the best interest of the child and award sole legal custody to one parent. That would be me," Rhett concluded. His words sounded rehearsed, as if he had been waiting to drop that news on Jade, and crush her with it. It was payback for the pain. And it was legal.

Sher was upstairs and had been out of earshot for what was going on downstairs in her living room. This was Jade's battle. She didn't have to fight it alone, but she wanted to take the first step right now with strength, dignity, and accept responsibility. Rhett was accustomed to seeing her shut down, or fly off the handle. Jade was determined not to do either right now. "So, I've been stripped of custody? That does not mean I cannot see my child, correct? Do you still plan to allow my family to be a part of her life? You've already said how my mother and Gram have saved you a time or two."

"I'm not saying you cannot visit with Aspen. If you're around when the ladies in your life are taking care of my daughter, I have no legal right to keep you from a play date here and there. You're just not a parent anymore to Aspen. You're no longer her mother." As Jade watched him standing before her, and heard his hateful words, she forced herself to look away. She willed herself to stay strong, and she looked at Aspen to gain strength. Aspen was bored with the toys in front of her and she was now jabbering as she walked closer to Jade, and that's when Jade enveloped her into her arms. She held her especially close and Aspen squealed and she snuggled against Jade's chest.

"Mommy will see you again, very soon," Jade said, capturing Aspen's attention, and then looking up, and making direct eye contact with Rhett as he stood on the floor in front of them.

Chapter 29

Jade spent the next week trying to find a job, a job that would look acceptable to a judge willing to modify the court document that granted Rhett sole legal custody of Aspen. She had to do everything possible to have the opportunity to raise her child. She wanted Rhett to agree to joint custody, but he refused. He used the excuse that she would just run again. It was his way of *protecting his daughter*.

So far, she had had no success finding a job. *No bars*, her mother had told her, *you're not going to make six figures overnight, but please stay away from tending bar again.* Jade then thought of Green Construction. She was going to make damn close to six figures, overnight, working for Karla. *Working*, Jade laughed to herself. She didn't miss Karla, that was for sure, but she did have Brock on her mind, day and night. He had not contacted her, and she was partly relieved. It would be too easy to run to him right now. He had rescued her once before, and she once again felt like she needed him, or someone, to tell her everything was going to be okay.

As she drove down Route 50 in her red Jeep, with the top down on a hot summer day, Jade saw the hotel where she lived with Brock for a couple of months. She felt such promise for the future when she was with him. And now the only thing she was looking forward to was raising her daughter. If that could happen. She had not seen Aspen in four days, but tomorrow she would again. Rhett had asked Sher to watch Aspen for a few hours. Jade really had no interest in knowing what Rhett's plans were, but she asked Sher anyway if she knew.

"He's seeing a woman, she's actually in the military," Sher told her. "The only thing he told me was she's home on leave because of a death in the family, otherwise she's stationed in Germany."

"Germany?" Jade had asked. "How do you date a woman who is going to pick up and go back to Europe?"

Sher had said she was not sure how serious the two of them were, but they were dating for nearly a month. It didn't bother Jade that Rhett was dating, but she felt worried about what could happen if their relationship turned serious.

Jade veered her Jeep toward the hotel. When she walked into the lobby, she caught the eye of the hotel manager, at the front desk. His name was Don. Jade had gotten to know him a little, while she lived there with Brock. He was a retired colonel in the military. His kids were grown, his grandchildren didn't live close by, and his wife was career driven, but he had never said what she did for a living.

"Well I'll be damned! Jade? I thought you were living in the South?" Don stood up from behind the desk, with his powder blue short-sleeved oxford shirt tucked tight around his round belly. Jade couldn't see the pant legs of his black pants, but she guessed they were too short and showing his white socks which he always wore with black tennis shoes. His wavy hair was snow white and his smile was wide.

"That didn't quite work out as planned," she answered, and left it at that.

"So you're back to live here for awhile and you need a room again? Your suite isn't vacant, but I can set you up in a regular room until it is," Don said, wiggling the mouse on his computer to wake up the file for the hotel's room availability.

"Oh, no, that's not why I'm here," Jade took his attention away from the computer again. "I was driving by, and I thought I'd take a chance and see if you have a job opening. I can do anything, office work, clean rooms, maintenance..."

"A pretty thing like you would look good sitting behind this desk," Don said to her. "I could give you my shift."

Jade didn't think he had a shift, he was the manager. She assumed someone must have quit, but she didn't ask because she didn't care. She was about to have a job. A job that might not pay much, but it was a start. "Are you serious? Don! You have no idea how much that would mean to me!"

"When can you start?" he asked her, and she almost threw her arms around his neck.

"Right now," she replied.

***

Jade spent three hours with Don, learning the ins and outs of working behind a hotel's front desk. She caught on quickly to the computer software and how to work the phone system. He also walked her to the back of the building to the housekeeping department so the staff could meet her. A few of them remembered her from when she temporarily lived there. Good thing she was always kind to everyone, Jade thought. She had left a good impression then and now it had paid off.

When a college student came to start her shift at the front desk, Don introduced Jade to her and then told Jade to return for the five to two-thirty shift tomorrow morning. He instructed her to dress nice and she giggled inside at the thought of him in his short pants and white socks.

Knowing Sher was still at school, Jade drove to see her grandmother first. She would have done so anyway, even if her mother was not working. Angie was the one person she ran to first, for everything. Good news. Bad news. To talk. To seek advice. Or, just to be with her.

Jade found her immediately in her garden. She was sitting sideways on her gardening knee pad, and digging carefully in the dirt with a trowel. She was wearing a faded pair of jean shorts which ended mid-thigh, and Jade noticed were frayed on the ends. Those shorts were most likely a pair of jeans in her closet at one time. Jade smiled, knowing Angie was one to log on to YouTube to watch a video on how to cut and fray a pair of jeans, making them into a stylish pair of cut-offs. Her sleeveless dark purple shirt was grubby from the soil and the matching flip flops on her feet were also dirt-covered. Angie was not afraid to get dirty. She discovered gardening to be a meaningful hobby in the later years of her life. It gave her a purpose to keep up with nature's beauty right there in her backyard. And, not to mention, Angie loved being out in the sun.

"Hi, Gram," Jade said, standing before her in a pretty yellow sundress with her dark brown ankle wrap sandals. Unlike Angie's, Jade's tanned skin had faded a bit as she had not been lying by the pool since that late afternoon at Brock's house when Karla showed up with wine.

"Oh, Jadey," I didn't notice you were here," Angie said, taking a few seconds to reposition her body on the ground so she could stand up. "Let's go sit down on the swing."

Angie led the way and Jade followed, sitting down right beside her. She had her garden gloves off and she was beating them together to knock off the dirt. She did the same with her flip flops before she put them back on her feet. Jade thought her grandmother was entirely too cute, and she smiled as she watched her, in silence. And then Angie turned to her.

"What's on your mind?" she asked Jade.

"Aspen," Jade answered, "and how I intend to do everything I can to get her back in my life."

"You will, eventually," Angie replied. "You just need to remember that sometimes we have to work toward things in life. Sometimes, something we want most is far from being handed to us. It may seem out of reach, or even not meant to be, but if you push and shove and claw your way, it will be worth it when you're there."

"You sound as if you have something you want to tell me," Jade said, knowing her best.

"I do," Angie stated. "See these new gardening gloves? I just bought them today. My other ones were worn and getting holes in them. I bumped into Dana Connors while I was at the store." Jade nodded her head. Dana Connors was her former mother-in-law. She did a wonderful job raising Rhett. She taught him how to be responsible and caring. He was a good father to Aspen, but he had not been so caring to Jade as of late. This custody deal was now tearing Jade apart. It had taken her too long to want to be a part of Aspen's life, and now Rhett was keeping her away. But, legally, Jade had high hopes for that to change very soon.

"She's always kind to me," Angie said, "and today she was very chatty. Are you aware that Rhett is dating an Air Force woman?"

"Yes, mom told me. I'm happy he's getting out, seeing someone, but I'm not sure if that's such a good idea. She's not stationed here at the Base, is she?"

"No. She's been living in Germany for three years and has at least one more to go before her next assignment." Angie knew a lot, Jade thought, just from one conversation with Dana Connors.

"Why is she on leave here?" Jade asked, just out of curiosity as she thought she remembered her mother saying something about a leave.

"Her father died," Angie replied, "and her mother is terribly lost right now. She's staying with her, trying to get her settled before she goes back to Germany."

"That's too bad," Jade said, not really understanding having a relationship with a father. Hers had always been distant and then after her parents divorced and he remarried a man, he cut himself out of her life. Jade's relationship with Sher was not much better, but they had at least been present in each other's lives. Living with her now was not the easiest arrangement, but Jade was grateful. And she was doing it in order to be able to frequently see Aspen. Otherwise, she would be living with her Gram. That was a relationship Jade understood. The two of them were connected like sisters, like mother and daughter, like two people who shared the same soul.

"Dana told me something, Jadey," Angie began, "and it's not good. But, before I tell you and before you react, I want you to remember what I just told you. We never give up on the things we want most in this life, even if we have to strive to make it happen."

"Gram, out with it. I am a big girl," Jade said, adamantly. "I have dealt with pain. I know heartbreak. I know disappointment. Hell, I survived a deadly overdose." Jade had a keen sense of humor and Angie smiled at her.

"Rhett is contemplating moving to Germany to be with this woman. Apparently, he's not concerned about being able to find employment, given how handy he is and now being experienced in plumbing. His parents always travel. His mother told me he has nothing holding him back."

"And he's planning to take Aspen with him?" Jade spoke calmly, at first. "To Europe?" she raised her voice. "My daughter will be halfway around the fucking world!" There it was. Jade's patience had run out, because she was suddenly scared. She could not allow Rhett to take her daughter away from her, not when she *finally* wanted to be her mother.

***

Jade was sitting on the front porch of the old blue house she used to share with Rhett. They never had outdoor furniture before, but there were now two dark brown wicker chairs with beige cushions and a small table centered between the two. Jade made herself comfortable and sat down in one of them. Rhett was not home from work yet, but he would be soon. She wondered if Aspen enjoyed going to the daycare center at the First Baptist Church. A lot of children were enrolled there, Sher had told her, and Rhett mentioned how happy Aspen seemed when he dropped her off and picked her up each day. It was a private daycare, but since Rhett's parents were members of the church, Aspen could attend. Rhett's parents were also paying for the tuition.

Jade had a lot to learn, still, about her daughter. She wanted to know everything. She wanted to be a part of it all. And now she was beyond worried it could be too late.

Minutes before she was expecting Rhett to pull up in his little charcoal gray pickup truck, Jade sat alone and thinking and trying like all hell not to feel hopeless. Then, as a black Chevrolet Traverse pulled up onto the driveway and behind the wheel was a woman, Jade sat up straighter in her chair. *This must be her.*

A woman, tall with red curly hair hanging loose and down to her shoulders got out of the vehicle wearing short white shorts. She was rail thin, as Jade often described Rhett. She had absolutely no curve to her body, her chest was flat, and her shoulders were broad, but bony in a red tank top. *Are redheads supposed to wear red?* Jade pondered. She wore a pair of white Keds slip-on tennis shoes, barefoot, and Jade watched her walk up onto the small porch where Jade sat, staring at her from behind in her large, dark sunglasses.

"Hello?" the woman spoke first.

"Hi, you must be Rhett's new lady love," Jade said, sounding annoyed. This was the woman behind Rhett's possible decision to leave the country, with Aspen.

"I'm Kelly," she responded. "And you must be the gem they call Jade." This woman knew how to dish it right back.

"I've been called worse," Jade smirked.

"Are you here to see Rhett?" Kelly asked, reaching into her purse for a key and then proceeding to unlock the door. If she had a key, their relationship was serious, Jade thought. *Well, of course it was serious!* She scolded herself. *Rhett wanted to move to Germany just to be with her!*

Jade got up off of the chair and followed her inside. "Yes, I will just wait for him, if you don't mind."

"Not at all," Kelly said, walking directly into the kitchen and Jade again followed. It was weird to be there. It was once her house, but never felt like much of a home. It was Aspen's home. And that was why Jade was back there again. This was about her daughter.

Jade could smell something cooking, and then she noticed Kelly walk over to a crock-pot on the counter. She lifted up the lid, stirred something inside with a large spoon. Jade recognized the spoon, but not much else. Especially not the fully-stocked refrigerator when Kelly opened it and offered her a bottle of water.

Jade accepted it, and spoke again. "Looks like you're making things awfully homey here. I'm happy Rhett has someone to take care of him." Jade wanted to add, *I was never any good at it,* but she refrained.

"Thank you," Kelly responded. "We're both very happy."

"Happy enough to invite him and my daughter to play house in Germany?" Jade asked, wanting to get to the point of why she was there. She should be discussing this with Rhett, but he wasn't there yet and she wasn't going to waste time talking about the weather.

"Yes," Kelly said. "My father just died. I've spent the past four weeks watching my mother try to pick up the pieces and live without him. She's lost. She loved him that much. The two of them taught me if you find happiness, seize it and then nurture it to keep it growing and lasting for as long as you are given life on this earth." Jade wondered why she was telling her so much. The more she spoke, the more Jade liked her, and she wasn't so sure if that was a good thing.

"I'm sorry about your father," Jade said.

"Me, too," Kelly responded.

"I'm sure you're still reeling from loss, so don't you think it's unwise to make any life-altering decisions for awhile? Asking Rhett to move that far away from his home, uprooting his child, is drastic."

"I agree," Kelly said, sitting down at the table adjacent from Jade's chair. "It was Rhett's idea."

"What?" Jade asked, entirely caught off guard.

"He's the one ready for change," Kelly explained, "and I'm not stopping him. I think I'm falling in love with him and I know I've already fallen for his daughter."

"She's my daughter, too," Jade said, feeling like she wanted to scream. But, who would she scream at? This woman in front of her for caring about Rhett? Rhett for continuing to love and take exceptional care of Aspen? It was herself she could have screamed at. It was her fault this was happening. She was the one who walked away.

Kelly only nodded her head, and tipped back the bottle of water she was drinking. Less than a second later, in walked Rhett. He was carrying Aspen until they reached the inside of the living room doorway. He then put her on her feet and she moved her little short legs swiftly into the kitchen. She must have known they had guests in their house.

Jade's face lit up when she saw her. She moved her chair back and prepared to stand up as Aspen continued to be on the move in her direction. Just as Jade wanted to grab ahold of her and squeeze her, because she had not seen her in four days, Aspen passed her by and ended up in Kelly's arms. "Hi sweetheart, how was your day? You look so pretty in your baby blue dress and white sandals." The two of them had a bond. Already. It was so painfully obvious, as Jade watched them. And then Rhett broke her total concentration by saying her name as she stared at her daughter with that woman. "Jade? What are you doing here?"

"We need to talk," she responded, still feeling the rippling effect of seeing *her* daughter being mothered by her ex-husband's girlfriend.

"I'll take Aspen, we'll play. Dinner will be ready when we are," Kelly said to Rhett as he smiled at her. It was one of those smiles with his eyes, and Jade could see he was happy. He cared about her. Probably even loved her already.

Jade managed to receive fleeting eye contact and then a shy smile from Aspen before she left the room with Kelly. Maybe she was only used to seeing her at Sher's house, Jade thought, but still felt pained. Rhett sat down at the table in the same chair Kelly had pulled out, and he waited for Jade to speak.

"I know about your tentative plans to leave the country with our daughter," she began. "I want you to be happy. You seem to be with Kelly, and it's obvious how much Aspen adores her. But, how is that fair to me? I am her mother and you can't take her that far away. You just can't."

"You are her mother," Rhett responded, "your name is on her birth certificate. But, you haven't been much of one." Jade sat there, listening, and taking in Rhett's words. He was right, but dammit she wanted a second chance! *Why did she have to be made to feel as if it were too late?*

Jade thought of Angie. She had been gone from the lives of her girls for four years, and still she returned and made a life with them. Circumstances were different from Jade's, but the scenario was the same. She was their mother. She deserved to be a part of her children's lives.

"No, I haven't," Jade agreed with him, "but I will be. Starting now. You just have to give me the chance. Work with me to get the custody agreement modified."

"I think you better go. I'm about to have dinner with my family," Rhett told her as he stood up from the table.

Jade's eyes widened. She thought, *you son of bitch*, but she kept calm. "I have a job now. I have a nice place to live. I have the support of my family. I will not let you win. I have rights, too." Jade stood up and she thought she saw a smirk on his face.

"I just gave my two-week's notice at Spengler. My parents will handle selling this house. No judge will turn this around in your favor that quickly. You might want to be around when I bring Aspen over to say goodbye to your mother and grandmother."

"You son of a bitch!" There, she said it. There was no holding back anymore. This fight was just beginning.

Chapter 30

Jade tried, but she couldn't get ahead of Rhett. Sher hired a lawyer for her and Jade pled her case. But, in turn, she was told it could take at least six months, or up to a year, before a hearing would be held to review the case. No judge would give her the time of day any sooner. Jade had to prove herself. She had merely been working for a few days, and back living in the same state as her daughter for two weeks. Nothing was going to change overnight. Rhett had sole legal custody and he was moving out of the country with Aspen.

Jade had found herself back there, back in that place where she believed the world was a cold, cruel place. Sher could not get through to her because of her own anger issues about losing Aspen. She had developed a real relationship with her only grandchild and now that would cease. Sher was angry with Rhett, but she was most furious with Jade. In her yes, she had screwed up yet again.

It was Angie, however, who believed this trying time would pass. She was a woman who had not gone through life unscathed, she knew how to power through the obstacles, and she refused to see any other outcome except for survival. She pushed Jade to do what she was told. *Listen to the lawyer. Work hard. Stay on course. Do not get discouraged. Prove yourself. Get your baby back. Maybe not today or tomorrow, but eventually you will.*

Jade's shift at the hotel ended at midnight. She had worked a double to fill in for the college student who could not be there. Jade walked to her Jeep, got in, and drove home to Sher's house with the windows down and the top off. The warm night air in her hair and on her face made her feel alive. She was thinking of Brock and the first night he bought her that Jeep and asked her to drive him around town in it. Damn, they were happy. And dammit, she missed him. He would never believe what she was going through right now. He was probably thinking she was living happily ever after, rebuilding her life with her baby girl. Jade wondered *if he had found someone else already. If he had forgiven his mother for destroying their relationship. If he missed her.* Jade cried herself to sleep a few hours later, missing him, and dreading saying goodbye to Aspen the following day, not knowing how long it would be before she would see her again.

***

As he said he would, Rhett showed up midday at Sher's house with Aspen. He had her dressed in a pale pink romper with sandals to match. Angie was at the house, too, and she, Sher and Jade were waiting in the living room when they arrived. Jade had not been crying in front of them, but she was terribly quiet. Angie had been the only one doing the talking.

Jade was the first to stand up and answer the door. Again, Rhett had been carrying Aspen, but put her on her feet to walk inside the house. She ran past Jade again and straight over to Sher. She knew her grandmother and the gesture alone of watching her lift her little arms high into the air for her, sent Sher's heart reeling. Little by little, this tiny, amazing creature she had gotten to know and grown to love would soon forget her. Sher knew that. She picked her up and held Aspen with both arms wrapped so tightly around her, and she closed her eyes to shut out the pain erupting inside of her. Aspen was jabbering and became antsy in Sher's arms, so Sher quickly looked at her, their eyes bore into each others, and she told her, "I love you, Aspen Angela. Never forget that." Jade had never heard her mother say those words. She just didn't express herself that way, or she had never with Jade. Sher couldn't take it anymore. She left. She took her handbag off of the sofa table against the wall and she didn't look back. She couldn't, because if she had, that little girl would have seen her falling apart.

Angie assumed Sher would go to her office. That is what she did. She threw herself into her career. It was easier that way. There, she had power, respect, and she loved the children, but kept them at arm's length. No one got hurt that way.

Angie was next. When Aspen walked over to her, sitting on the end of the couch, she found her favorite plush monkey on her lap. Angie kept toys for Aspen at her house and that particular monkey was her favorite. She brought it today. She wanted to give it to Aspen to take along with her, to her new home. "This is yours to keep. Take it with you when you and your daddy move." Aspen smiled and picked up the monkey and held it close to her face. If she squeezed it any harder, the stuffing may have popped out. Angie lifted Aspen up onto her lap. "You are a such a good girl. You are so loved. Come home to us soon." Aspen clearly repeated *home* and Angie squeezed her tiny, but chubby hand, and then put both of her own seventy-five-year-old hands on the sides of Aspen's baby face. She loved her so. When she moved off of Angie's lap, Angie slowly took steps to leave the living room. Before she completely exited the room, she turned and looked back, directly at Rhett. "You're not doing the right thing," she told him. "This will come back to bite you in the ass one day, I promise you that, Rhett Connors." He never said a word in response.

Angie stayed in the house, in the kitchen. She wanted to give the three of them their privacy, but she also wanted to be there for Jade. Jade was the last person left in the living room and Aspen made her way over to her. Jade couldn't help but think how Aspen must feel. She didn't know her own mother. She didn't run to her first, because she never felt loved by her. *Maybe it was too late*, Jade thought. *Maybe it was time to completely let go, forever.*

Jade picked her up, pulling her close and trying her damndest to be strong. "Do the two of you need a ride to the airport?" Jade asked, looking at Rhett, hoping he would say yes, hoping she could buy a little more time with her little girl.

"No, my parents have that covered," he replied.

"Is Kelly already there?" Jade asked, wondering if they were traveling as a *family*.

"She's been back in Germany for a week already," he answered.

"I hope you will be happy with her, and there, in a strange country." This was turning into small talk. Again, she was trying to stall. She wanted more time.

"Jade, we have to go," he said, adamantly. "Tell her goodbye."

The tears welled up in Jade's eyes. The lump in her throat kept getting larger. She was trembling as Aspen stared with interest. "My baby girl," she began, as her bottom lip trembled and the tears sprung from her eyes. "God didn't give you the best mother, and I'm so sorry, you'll never know how sorry I'll always be, for not giving you what you needed. I will always carry you with me. I love you, oh God, I love you." Jade was choking on her sobs.

Angie was standing in the doorway between the kitchen and the open living room, and she was listening. She had a tissue wadded up in her aging hand and she continued to dab the tears as they free fell onto her face. She had her share of pain in her lifetime, but this was going to be the death of her. She was certain of it. If things did not turn around in Jade's favor, their family was sure to fall apart. Sher would lose herself in hatred again. Jade would sink into depression. And, Angie, would do something she's never fathomed doing before. Give up. For the first time in her life, she felt too old to handle it all.

She left the doorway and walked over to the kitchen table. She reached into the pocket of her white denim capris and found her cell phone. She checked for any missed calls or messages and there were none. And, then she spoke aloud, "Time is running out. Do something, and do it now."

Back in the living room, Jade began to cry harder as Rhett stepped toward her and took Aspen out of her arms. "Mama?" Jade heard her say those words so clearly. She knew. Aspen knew of her as her *mama*. She was happy to have that moment, that truth, to carry with her now. But, it saddened her, too, knowing her daughter would remember her mother as nonexistent.

Jade followed them out of the house. She stood on the spacious front porch, with stamped concrete, in a white sundress and bare feet. Her hair was down and reached her shoulders, and she had one hand covering her mouth, attempting to muffle her sobs. She forced herself to watch them leave. Aspen waved three times, and Jade responded to each and every one. *She used to cry and I didn't pick her up. She used to babble and I didn't talk to her. She used to want to play and I ignored her. She used to need me and want me, but now she never will again.*

Jade was breaking inside. This moment would forever be frozen in her mind. She blamed herself, and always would. As Rhett closed the back door of his pickup truck, after getting Aspen into her car seat, he opened the driver's side door and got in. Jade heard him start the engine while she focused on her little girl in the back seat. She could see her blonde curls, her wide eyes, and then she heard the roar of a vehicle speeding down the road. It was coming toward them as Rhett began to back out of the driveway. She watched Rhett slam on his breaks as the truck on the road did the same, blocking the end of the driveway.

Jade would know that own-the-road truck anywhere. Her heart felt as if it suddenly skipped a beat. She watched him get out of the truck and run up the driveway. Brock Green never looked so good to her. But, she had no idea why he was there. He was carrying something in his hand and he used his other hand to open Rhett's truck door. Rhett got out and stood up to him. Jade made her way off of the porch and down the driveway just as she heard Rhett say, "What the hell are you doing?" to Brock.

"Delivering the official court documents to keep your ass and that precious baby girl in the country," Brock replied, shoving the papers against Rhett's chest. "Read for yourself. You and Jade now have joint legal custody of Aspen."

As Rhett forced his eyes on the document, Jade reached Brock's side. He turned to her and smiled. His face, his eyes, were lit. God, she loved him. "What did you do? How did you even know?" Jade had questions and in due time Brock would give her all of the answers she needed. Now, he only looked up at the front porch and smiled at the woman Jade called *Gram*.

EPILOGUE

Jade sped down Lincoln Street all the way to the outskirts of town. She finally made a left turn onto their property as she thought about all the years she had lived in O'Fallon and that land was just acres upon acres of field. It may have been farmland once upon a time, but she only knew of it as just an endless field of weeds. Now, on it, was an estate, an exact replica of what Brock had owned in Franklin, Tennessee. He said he built the house the same, but Jade could have sworn this one was larger. The land was exactly as she had remembered though, complete with the barn, the lake, the gazebo, and the swimming pool. This was home. This estate was theirs.

Two years ago, Brock left his life in Franklin, Tennessee behind. After Jade left, he knew none of it mattered anymore without her. He started to make plans. He quit his position as vice president of Green Construction, packed his truck full of what he wanted to take with him, and left the rest behind. He moved back into the suite of that hotel just off of Interstate 64 in O'Fallon, Illinois. He parked his truck behind the back of the building, and he rarely left his hotel suite. He stayed there, working tirelessly day and night, on the computer, on the phone, and he began to launch a new company. This one was solely his, and it would be called Jade Construction. He didn't care if he made millions as he had with his family's company in Tennessee. He only hoped to carry on what he believed in, and that was, above all, giving his customers superior quality.

His return was planned to be a surprise for Jade, but Brock was the one who ended up taken aback when Don, the manager of the hotel, informed him about Jade working there. He was aware of her custody struggle and the slim chance of Jade ever getting to raise her daughter who was leaving the country, and he shared all of it with Brock.

It was then that Brock reached out to Angie, and the two of them worked together to save Jade from losing Aspen. It was twenty-four hours before Rhett and Aspen were set to leave the country when Angie hurried to contact the lawyer Jade had hired. Then, Brock arranged for all of the documents from that lawyer to be sent to a judge in Tennessee, who owed the Green family a favor. The policy originally forcing Jade to wait six months to a year before a hearing would be held to review the custody case was waived. Jade no longer had to prove herself fit to be Aspen's mother. Brock handled that and ensured Rhett would no longer have sole legal custody, which meant he would be stopped from moving out of the country with Aspen. Brock rescued Jade, once again.

Jade got out of her Jeep after having parked it close to the house. Then, she looked down the lane road and saw the school bus coming. *Perfect timing*, she sighed in relief. She waited for the bus to drive up to the paved circle in front of their house. After it came to a halt, the door opened, and a smiling three-year-old Aspen, with her backpack strapped on her back, descended the steps and pounced into Jade's arms. She was happy to be home from her first day of preschool. And Jade was overjoyed that this was her scheduled week to care for Aspen. She and Rhett rotated every seven days with her. When Aspen was not living at the estate with Jade and Brock, she lived in town with her daddy and his wife, Kelly.

Aspen knew she was not part of a typical family. Hers had imperfections. She had a mommy and a daddy, but they did not live together, because they loved Brock and Kelly. She had a Grandma Sher who *loved her to the moon and back* and told her so every chance she got. And, then there was Great Gram. That lady was special. Even Aspen knew it. She was the glue that held their family together.

About the Author

With each book I write, there has always been a story behind the story, or an inspiring moment which sets off the storyline in my mind, like wildfire.

For this book, I knew I wanted to create characters with imperfections. No one is perfect, of course, but some of us appear to be more put together than others. Appear is the key word. We don't know what goes on in other people's lives. Unless we really know people, we have no idea of their stress, their heartache, their need or desire to do something drastic as a last resort to embrace change and save themselves. Or find peace.

One of my favorite quotes is, "Be kind to one another, because you never know what battles people are fighting." I created a character (Jade) in this book with hope for readers to like her, and root for her, despite the awful choice she made. It was riveting for me to write about her and still like her, and accept her.

We all have flaws and we each have those people in our lives who accept us for who we are. Those people often times save us. Without them, we believe we could not carry on. Those people are beacons. My hope for you all this time, as I publish my sixth book, is for you to recognize those beacons in your life, or to be one for someone else.

As always, thank you for reading!

love,

Lori Bell

Made in the USA
Middletown, DE
08 August 2015